MYTH O MANIA

VII

UNDERWORLD LIBRARY
ANCIENT GREECE

AUTHOR
Kate McMullan

TITLE
Get to Work, Hercules!

DATE DUE	BORROWER'S NAME
XXVII	*Lord Hades*
XXXI	*Lord Hades*

Myth-O-Mania is published by Stone Arch Books
A Capstone Imprint
1710 Roe Crest Drive
North Mankato, Minnesota 56003
www.capstonepub.com

*Library of Congress Cataloging-in-Publication Data is available on the
Library of Congress website.*

Library binding: 978-1-4342-3196-3 · Paperback: 978-1-4342-3440-7

Summary: Hades reveals the truth behind the story of Hercules and his labors.

Cover Character Illustration: Denis Zilber
Cover, Map, and Interior Design: Bob Lentz
Production Specialist: Michelle Biedscheid

Image Credits:
Shutterstock: 1xpert, bioraven, B. McQueen, Cre8tive Images, Mclek,
Natalia Barsukova, NY-P, osov, Pablo H Caridad, Perov Stanislav,
Petrov Stanislav Eduardovich, Selena. Author photo: Phill Lehans.

Printed in the United States of America in Stevens Point, Wisconsin.
062013 007572R

MYTH-O-MANIA
VII

GET TO WORK, HERCULES!

BY
KATE McMULLAN

STONE ARCH BOOKS
a capstone imprint

THE XII LABORS OF HERCULES

TABLE of CONTENTS

PROLOGUE

Yep, it's me again, K.H.R.O.T.U. — King Hades, Ruler of the Underworld. I'm back to let you in on the T.R.U.T.H. — the Totally Real Unadulterated Trustworthy History — of another Greek myth.

Until I came along, I'll bet everything you knew about the myths was one big F.I.B. — Factually Inaccurate Bull-hooey. For that, you can thank my little brother, The Brave And Mighty Zeus — T-BAMZ for short. Zeus is the slimiest myth-o-maniac (old Greek speak for "liar liar pants on fire") in the world. No, make that the universe. Zeus lies in the A.M. He lies in the P.M. He'd lie to the F.B.I. and the C.I.A. if he had half a chance. And for sure he lied when he put together his version of *T.B.F.B.O.G.M.*, *The Big Fat Book of Greek Myths*. You've heard of the hero, Hercules, right? Check out the Zeus-approved version of the myth about him. Go on, read it straight from the pages of the *B.F.B.O.G.M.*:

HERCULES WAS THE MORTAL SON OF ZEUS. LIKE ZEUS, HE HAD THE COURAGE OF A LION AND THE STRENGTH OF A BULL. HE WAS GIVEN XII LABORS. EACH ONE WOULD HAVE BEEN IMPOSSIBLE FOR A NORMAL MORTAL. BUT HERCULES DID ALL XII. HERCULES WAS THE GREATEST HERO GREECE HAS EVER KNOWN.

Zeus makes it sound as if Hercules did the twelve labors all by himself. Not a chance. Hercules was strong all right. He had great big muscles. But he had an itty-bitty brain. The T.R.U.T.H. is, if it hadn't been for a certain street-smart lion, a loyal nine-headed monster, and a quick-thinking Ruler of the Underworld, Hercules wouldn't have made it past Labor I. Here's another bit of T.R.U.T.H. for you: big muscles can only do so much. Without brains, muscles are just . . . well, bulgy things in your arms and legs.

In addition to big muscles, Hercules also had a big temper. It got him into some mighty big trouble. Who do you think helped Hercules out of all the jams he got himself into? Take a wild guess. It wasn't T-BAMZ. No, Zeus was too busy hurling T-bolts and making proclamations. He never took the time to give the kid a hand. The T.R.U.T.H. is, it was always U.H.T.T.R. — Uncle Hades To The Rescue.

Sit down. Put your feet up. Let me tell you the *real* story of Hercules. I remember everything about the night that great big baby was born. . . .

Chapter 1
BIG BABY

"Stare that Centaur down, Cyclops!" I chanted as I boogied over to pick up my Helmet of Darkness. I put it on, and — *POOF!* I vanished.

I, Hades, Ruler of the Underworld, was dancing around my palace. Not that dignified, maybe, but that night, I was too excited about the big wrestling match at Palace Stadium to sit still. The winner would earn the Wrestling Immortals Championship Girdle — (old speak for "belt"). "Eagle-Eye" Cyclops, the One-Eyed Giant, was up against "Half 'n' Half" Centaur, who was part man, part horse. As always, I had my money on the big one-eyed guy.

I kept on chanting — "You can make him blink, Cyclops!" — as I tossed my helmet into my

K.H.R.O.T.U. wallet. It's a magical wallet, and it
expands to hold whatever I put inside. Then it
shrinks back down to fit in my pocket. Nice, huh?

Next, I bopped down to the kitchen. I tossed
some Ambro-Salt and a couple of cans of Necta-
Cola into the wallet, too. Ambrosia and nectar —
the food and drink of the gods. That's what keeps
us young and good-looking — forever! Now,
whatever mortal food I might have to eat, I could
sprinkle on a little Ambro-Salt, chug a Necta-
Cola, and turn it into a meal fit for a god.

"Go, Cyclops, go!" I chanted, doing a little
spin.

I'd made the rounds of my Underworld
kingdom earlier that evening. Everything was
shipshape. My queen, Persephone, goddess of
spring, was working up on earth, making the
flowers bloom. So I had nothing better to do than
head up to Palace Stadium in Thebes to catch
the big match. I grabbed a slice of leftover pizza
from the fridge and headed out into the night.
Cerberus, my three-headed guard dog, trotted at
my heels.

"Woof! Woof! Woof?" he barked as I made a beeline for the royal stables.

"No, you have to stay here tonight, Cerbie," I told him.

"Awoooo!" his third head howled in protest.

That head had started acting up lately. I made a mental note to give it a little extra training when I got back.

"You have to guard my kingdom, Cerbie," I said. "That's your job!"

My dog turned his back on me and sat down in protest. I knew he'd get over it, so I continued on my way to the stables. I hitched my steeds, Harley and Davidson, to my sportiest little chariot and drove up to earth.

Back in the old days, the trip took me nine days. But now, thanks to the shortcut that Cerberus had shown me, I could get up to earth in only a few hours. That night, I made great time. Before long, I drove out of a cave, and I was on earth.

I parked in the usual lot near Athens. Then I began chanting the astro-traveling spell. This is a little plus of being a god. When we're on earth, all we have to do is recite a certain godly spell containing the ZIP code of where we want to go, and — *ZIP!* — we're there. And so I chanted a spell for Palace Stadium.

ZIP!

I looked around. I had expected to see wrestlers and trainers and hordes of loyal fans waving pennants and yelling, "Kill him, Cyclops!"

Instead, I found myself in a deserted room. It had marble floors and tiny little windows way up high on the walls. I started walking. A few flickering lanterns lit the hallways. It took me a moment to realize what had happened. By some astro-traveling mix-up, instead of going to Palace Stadium, I'd landed in the basement of the royal palace of Thebes.

I chanted the spell again.

ZIP!

I stayed right where I was.

I figured the astro-traveling network was down. I decided to make my way out of the royal palace and try again. I hurried up a staircase to my left and reached a landing. I heard voices. Quickly, I took my helmet from my wallet. I put it on. *POOF!* No one could see me now.

I tiptoed to the room where I'd heard the voices. I stuck my invisible head in at the door. A nursemaid was holding a bundle wrapped in a blanket. She was showing the bundle to a young mortal woman sitting up in a bed. That young woman — I'd met her somewhere, I was sure of it. But where? I couldn't think.

"Rejoice, Princess Alcmene," said the nursemaid, holding up what turned out to be a great big baby. "It's a boy!"

Alcmene? I knew that name. But who *was* she?

I was about to tiptoe away when the princess spoke.

"A boy?" she said. "Oh, dear."

I stopped. In those days, everyone wanted boy babies. It made no sense, even way back then, but that's how it was. So I waited to find out why this princess was unhappy to have a boy.

"Be glad!" said the nurse. "He is big and strong. He looks like a child of a god."

"He *is* the child of a god," said Princess Alcmene. "His father is Zeus, remember?"

Zeus? Ye gods! Was there nowhere I could go without hearing his blasted name?

It all came flooding back to me then. Of course I'd met Alcmene — at her wedding to my little brother. She and Zeus had been married for only a short time. But it was evidently long enough for Zeus to have fathered a son. And if this was Zeus's son, that made the great big baby my nephew. I was his uncle!

Of course Zeus's main hobby was founding a Zeus Dynasty. He had hundreds of children. Which meant that I had hundreds of nieces and nephews. But I'd never seen any of them when they were this brand new. Uncle Hades. I liked the sound of it.

"Suns and moons!" exclaimed the nursemaid. "Zeus is married to Hera now. She hates Zeus's children by his former wives. Especially his sons."

That was the truth. Hera was Queen of the

Universe now. She had it all. But she was still jealous of Zeus's exes and their offspring.

"I know," the princess said sadly. "We cannot risk Hera's jealous rage. She might destroy all of Thebes. Quick, take the baby to that peasant woman who sews for me. She has twelve children of her own. Surely she won't mind one more. Ask her to care for him until we figure out what to do."

The nursemaid nodded. She wrapped another blanket around the big baby. Then she held him out to his mother for a kiss. I flattened myself against the wall as the nurse rushed past me out of the room.

"You're a heavy bundle, you are," she said to the big baby as she went by.

I hurried after her. When I'm invisible, I always try to find someone to follow. That way I don't have to worry about anyone seeing doors that seem to open on their own.

I followed that nursemaid, down the hallway and out of the palace. Once outside, I began chanting the astro-traveling spell to take me to the wrestling match. But halfway through, I stopped. I wanted to make sure that great big baby got where he was going. The kid was my nephew, after all. And besides, Cyclops was a star. There would be some warm-up matches before it was his turn to step into the ring. I had time to wait and see that the big baby ended up in the right hands.

I tailed the nursemaid through the winding streets of Thebes and out the city gates. A full moon shone that night, lighting our way. Far down the road, I saw the lights of Palace Stadium. The sight made me weak in the knees. I had to get there in time to see Cyclops put Centaur in a quadruple-leg hold.

I decided I could trust the nursemaid to deliver the big baby safely to the peasant, after all. I'd just started chanting again when the baby began to fuss.

"Stars and comets!" said the nursemaid. "Don't tell me you're hungry."

The big baby kept fussing.

"Great constellations!" the nursemaid

exclaimed. "I must find you some milk." She peered into the field beside the road. In the far corner, some cows lay sleeping.

"I'll move faster without you," said the nursemaid as she put the big fussy baby down in the tall grass by the side of the road. "I'll be back with some milk." And off she ran toward the cows.

I wanted to call after her. I mean, you don't just leave a new baby lying on the side of the road! But she was already out of sight.

Now the big baby stopped fussing and started crying for real.

His screeching was awful. I put my hands over my sensitive godly ears.

A cloud passed over the moon. I looked down the road. The torches of Palace Stadium glowed in the distance.

I looked down at the big baby. His mouth was wide open. He was really wailing now. I'd never spent so much time with a just-born baby. I didn't know what to do. But I knew I couldn't go off and leave him there bawling.

I sat down beside the big baby.

"Be quiet," I told him, in the nicest possible way.

He kept crying.

I was invisible. So the baby didn't know his Uncle Hades was there. He went on screaming.

I stuck out a finger and tickled him under the chin. He stopped crying. I tickled him some more. He started making happy, burbling sounds.

The nursemaid would be back soon, I told myself as I tickled. The second she returned, I'd start chanting. I'd definitely get to the stadium in time to see Eagle-Eye body-slam ol' Half 'n' Half.

I kept tickling that big baby. He looked like Zeus all right. Puffy cheeks. Rolls of fat on his neck. Not that there was much neck. Not much hair, either. But on a baby, it all looked sort of cute.

I walked my fingers down the big baby's chest and started tickling his tummy. Me, Hades, dreaded Ruler of the Underworld, going "Kitchy-kitchy-coo!" I couldn't believe it.

The big baby's cooing and burbling made me forget to keep my guard up. I never saw anyone coming down the road. The first thing I heard was a voice saying, "Look! A baby!"

I glanced up.

Ye gods!

It was Hera!

CHAPTER II

BIG BANG

Hera stood above me, staring down at the great big baby. Her best girlfriend of the moment, Athena, the goddess of wisdom, stood right beside her.

Oh, was I glad I was invisible. So, so glad! Hera looked about as friendly as a viper. Athena may be goddess of wisdom. But she's also goddess of war. She was dressed, as always, in a full suit of armor, complete with helmet. She's not exactly a goddess you'd want to meet on a lonely road at night.

Hera bent down and picked up the great big baby. "He's heavy!" she said. She eyed him closely. "He looks like someone I know."

"Oh, all babies look alike," said Athena.

Hera frowned. "No, he definitely reminds me of someone. But who?"

Athena whisked the big baby from Hera's arms. "Let's take him to that city over there and find him a nursemaid before he starts squalling."

The baby's real nursemaid was hiding behind an olive tree, watching. Clearly she wasn't willing to tangle with these two powerful immortals. Who could blame her?

The goddesses carried the big baby toward Thebes. I didn't trust Hera one bit. So, with a last longing look at Palace Stadium, I took off after them. They went straight to the royal palace. They brushed past the servants and took the baby right to Princess Alcmene.

"We found this big baby by the side of the road," Athena said. "Take care of him, will you? He may amount to something one day."

The princess could barely hide her joy as she took back her baby.

"I've got it!" Hera exclaimed suddenly. "He looks just like my husband! Why, if this is Zeus's baby, I'll —"

Athena grabbed Hera's elbow. "Let's go home and see if anyone is sacrificing any bulls to us tonight."

Hera took one last look at the baby. "He *is* Zeus's son," she hissed. "I can tell!"

Hera liked fragrant bull-sacrifice smoke as much as any goddess, so she let Athena yank her away. But Hera looked back. I could tell from her face that she was planning something special for that baby. And it wasn't any birthday party, either.

The big baby was in danger. I decided to stick around. Because by this time, I, Uncle Hades, had grown fond of the kid. Okay, he was Zeus's son. But he was a mere mortal. T-BAMZ would never pay any attention to him, that was for sure. My queen, Persephone, lived down in the Underworld with me for only three months a year. We'd decided that our odd living arrangements would make it hard to raise a family, so we had no children of our own. This big baby was my blood relative. He was as close as I was likely to get to having a son.

I also knew that when it came to revenge, no one held a candle to Hera.

So I stayed in the nursery that night, watching invisibly over Princess Alcmene and the big baby. I looked out the nursery window. I saw the Palace Stadium torchlights blink out. I wondered who'd won the big match. I hoped Eagle-Eye had pinned Half 'n' Half's flank to the mat.

"Close your eyes, little baby," sang Princess Alcmene softly. "I mean, close your eyes, big baby."

"Goo-ga!" burbled the big baby as Princess Alcmene tiptoed from the room. He wasn't one bit sleepy.

I listened to the big baby gooing and gaaing. I also listened to my stomach growling. A single slice of leftover pizza isn't exactly a dinner fit for a god. I was growing weak from hunger! Around midnight, I decided to make a quick dash into Thebes to get a bite. I knew the perfect spot — a fast-service all-night Greek diner. Hey, a god's got to eat! I astro-traveled to the diner and ordered a shish kebab.

"Would you like some fries with that?" the counter mortal asked.

"Definitely," I told him. "Just make it fast, will you?"

My order came in no time. I sprinkled on the Ambro-Salt, chugged down one of my Necta-Colas, and astro-traveled straight back to the palace. *ZIP!* I landed on the steps, and my godly ears were filled with the sound of a horrible, ichor-freezing scream. (Ichor — it's what we gods have instead of blood.)

I raced to the nursery, not bothering with my helmet. The nursemaid stood in the doorway, shrieking. I dodged past her and into the room. I saw why she was screaming.

Two big blue serpents had managed to slither into the cradle. They had wound themselves around the big baby's neck. They were trying to choke the life out of him!

The princess ran into the nursery. She began screaming even louder than the nursemaid.

The palace guards rushed in behind her, their torches blazing. They drew their swords.

But at the cradle, they stopped.

They were too late.

The baby gripped the throat of one big blue serpent in his left hand. In his right, he gripped the throat of the other. He was waving the snakes around like playthings.

"Goo-goo ga-ga!" he cooed. Then: BANG! He knocked the snakes together. When their heads met, the serpents sank their venomous fangs into each other's necks. The baby tossed them to the floor, stone dead.

"Nice work, kid!" I said.

Princess Alcmene turned. "Hades?" she said, clearly startled. "What are you doing here?"

"I, uh, had a little astro-traveling mix-up," I said, and I told her how I'd ended up in her palace. And how I'd heard Hera's threat. "I thought I'd stick around and make sure no harm came to your baby."

"Thank you, Hades," said Princess Alcmene. "When I was married to Zeus, you always were my favorite brother-in-law."

"Not that the kid needed any help," I added.

"He's a born wrestler. Not even a day old yet and he's already won his first match."

Princess Alcmene looked very proud. Then she frowned. "We've never had a snake problem in the palace," she said. "I wonder if I should call an exterminator."

"Don't bother," I told her. "Hera sent those serpents. You know how she feels about Zeus's sons by his former wives."

Princess Alcmene sighed. "My baby will be in constant danger. Will you watch over him, Hades?"

"I . . . uh . . . " I looked from her to the big baby. He was gooing and gaaing up a storm. I hadn't noticed before — he had dimples. Adorable! What is it about babies that makes them so hard to resist?

"You are his uncle, after all," added the princess.

"All right," I said. "I'll try to protect him from Hera. But I can't guarantee that I'll be successful. Hera is one tough baklava." I thought for a moment. "Have you given the baby a name?"

"No," said Alcmene. "I can't decide between Chickapeckeus and Duckawaddleus."

"Heavy-duty names, Alcmene," I said. "You know, I think Hera might let up on your baby if you named him after her."

"You're joking, right?" said the princess.

"No joke," I said. "It's the sort of thing we gods and goddesses take very seriously. What about calling him Heracles? It means 'for the glory of Hera.'"

Princess Alcmene groaned. "I can't, Hades," she said. "I just can't. Every time I say his name, I'll think of that horrible goddess."

"Shhhh!" I cautioned her. "She might have one of her spies listening." I thought for a moment. "I know. You can call him by the Roman version of the name — Hercules."

"Hercules." The princess smiled. "That has a nice ring to it. All right, Hades. Hercules it is."

I smiled, too. I'd just named my first baby!

CHAPTER III
BIG BOO-BOO!

The very next week, I went up to Mount Olympus. It was the last thing I wanted to do. But a promise is a promise, and I'd promised to help Hercules. I went straight to the ridiculously oversized palace where Hera lived. I told the door-opening nymphs I wanted to talk to Hera, and they showed me into the sitting room.

Hera took her time, but at last she came into the room, all smiles. "Hades!" she said. "So good to see you."

"You too, Hera," I said. "Listen, I've got some very nice news for you."

Hera sat down. "Tell me," she said. "I could use some good news. I've just had this huge fight with Artemis. I found her hunting right outside one of my temples! I mean, if she has to stalk around in the woods half naked with her bow and arrows all the time, which apparently she does, can't she do it outside one of her own temples?" Hera let out a big sigh. "Anyway, Hades, tell me the good news."

"Well, remember that big baby?" I said. "The one you and Athena found on the side of the road?"

Hera's smile quickly vanished. "I'll get that big baby," she growled.

"No, listen," I said quickly. "The baby's mother worships you, Hera. She is so sorry she offended you. Not that it's her fault, exactly," I added. "But she wanted to find a way to make it up to you. And so she has named her baby in your honor."

"She named her boy Hera?"

"No," I said. "She named him Hercules. It's Roman. It means 'for the glory of Hera.'"

Hera stared at me, unsmiling. She folded her arms across her chest. "Is that your nice news, Hades?"

I nodded. "It's not every day you get a baby named to glorify you, is it?"

"Oh, go tell it to Zeus," Hera said. "He'd probably believe you. But not me, Hades. I can see through your clever little scheme." She stood up. "And I'm still going to get that baby!" She whirled around and marched off in a huff. She left me sitting there wishing I'd let Princess Alcmene name the boy Chickapeckeus.

Now I was *really* worried about Hercules. Whenever Persephone was away, I dashed up to Thebes to check on him. And since Persephone lives up on earth for nine months of the year, I was up in Thebes quite a bit. Sometimes I put on my Helmet of Darkness and just checked to make sure Hercules was okay. But other times, I left off the helmet and hung out with the little guy. He was cute, even if he did look a lot like Zeus. And when he called me Uncle Hades, I have to say, it warmed my godly heart.

Princess Alcmene was a lovely young mortal, and before long she married again. This time she picked a nice, steady mortal for a husband,

Amphitryon. Of course, Princess Alcmene told her new husband that Hercules was Zeus's son. She told Hercules, too, even thought the boy was much too young to understand what having T-BAMZ for a dad really meant.

Amphitryon was fond of his stepson. And he could see that with the right training, such a big strong toddler could become a big strong hero. So when Hercules turned five, Amphitryon decided to give him a hero's education.

Amphitryon called on experts from all over the world to come and train young Hercules. If he'd asked me, I would have told him just to get the kid a couple of good wrestling partners. But he didn't ask. So I kept my mouth shut.

One teacher showed Hercules how to race a chariot. One showed him how to shoot a bow and arrow. One taught him boxing. One trained him in long-distance running. Finally one came who taught him to wrestle. I was glad about that! Another teacher taught him how to lead an army into battle. Hercules loved all this physical training. He learned quickly. He was so big and strong that he soon out-raced, out-shot, out-boxed, out-ran, out-wrestled, and out-led-into-battle all his teachers.

Amphitryon wanted young Hercules to have a well-balanced education, so he also hired tutors to teach him how to read, write, count, write poetry, sing, and play charades. Hercules was okay at charades, but he wasn't exactly a whiz at the sit-down-at-a-desk exercises. He did learn to count up to X. And if he took off his shoes, he could count up to XX. He read *Froggius and Toadius* all the way to the last page. Eventually he learned to write and even made up a few poems. This one is my favorite:

> Zeus is my Dad.
> I call him my pappy.
> He has lots of thunderbolts.
> I hope he won't zap me.
> — by Hercules, age 6½

But when it came to singing, Hercules was a disaster. And he knew it.

Princess Alcmene and Amphitryon seemed very disappointed that the boy couldn't learn to sing. So, on a day when I knew Zeus was away on business, I went up to Mount Olympus again. This time I went to see Polyhymnia, the muse of music.

"Hey, Poly," I said when I found her just outside her muse bungalow. She was standing atop a little hill, practicing her scales.

"*Do re mi fa so la ti* — Hades!" sang Polyhymnia. "What brings you here to see *mi-mi-mi*?"

I sat down on a bench nearby. "My nephew, Hercules," I told her. "He's Zeus's son, actually. Not that Zeus gives a fig one way or the other. Hercules is studying singing, but the boy can't carry a tune in a bucket. Maybe he could learn, though. He's only seven. You think there's anything you could do to help him?"

"If anyone can help him, it's *mi-mi-mi-mi-mi!*" sang Polyhymnia.

I told her when Hercules's next singing lesson was, and on the appointed day, Polyhymnia dropped by the palace music room. I was there, too. I didn't want Hercules to feel too much pressure, so I wore my helmet.

"All right, my boy," said his music teacher, Linus. "Start warming up your voice."

Hercules opened his mouth and sang, "*Augggghhhhhh!*"

That was all it took to send Polyhymnia running from the room with her hands over her ears. I caught up with her just before she ran out the gates of Thebes. I persuaded her to come and sit with me at a little café and calm down.

"*Do-do-do-do*-don't ever let him sing again!" she sang as the waiter brought our cappuccinos. "He sounds just like his *fa-fa-fa-fa*-father."

"Zeus is tone deaf?" I asked. Who knew? "So there's nothing you can do?"

"*Fa-fa-fa-fa-fa*-fahgeddaboutit!" sang Polyhymnia.

But Linus refused to give up on his pupil. Twice a week he came to the palace to give Hercules his singing lessons. I happened to be there for the very last one.

"*Do re me fa so la ti do!*" sang Linus as he plucked the strings of his lyre. "Now you try it, Hercules."

"It's time for my archery lesson," said Hercules.

"First, the scales," said Linus.

"Oh, dang," said Hercules.

"Sing NOW!" ordered Linus.

Hercules drew a deep breath and sang: "*Do re me fa fee foe foo!*"

"No!" Linus cried. He drew back his hand and slapped Hercules right across the face.

BIG boo-boo!

No one had ever hit Hercules before. His eyes flashed with anger. His chubby face turned bright red. He grabbed Linus's lyre and heaved it at his teacher, knocking him flat.

"Oops!" said Hercules, when he realized what he'd done. He quickly picked up his teacher — even at age seven, he was that strong — and carried him through the palace to his old nursemaid.

The nursemaid looked at the big bump rising around Linus's left eye.

"He'll live," she said. "But he's going to have quite a shiner."

Finally Linus came to. "Ooooh," he moaned. "Uh, sorry about slapping you, Hercules."

"Sorry about bonking you with the lyre," said Hercules. "It was an accident — sort of."

The two forgave each other.

But Linus was never quite the same after that. He took to wearing a dead fish over his left eye. He said its scales reminded him never to make Hercules sing *his* scales if he didn't want to.

CHAPTER IV
BIG TATTLETALE

Hercules kept growing bigger and stronger. Most of the time, he was a kindhearted boy. But when Hercules got angry, "accidents" seemed to happen.

I stopped by the palace one afternoon when Hercules was around nine. I only meant to stay a couple of minutes, so I had on my helmet.

Princess Alcmene was out on the royal lawn with her son and his cousin, Eurystheus. Hercules was big, brawny, and healthy. Eury was pale, scrawny, and had a seriously runny nose. The boys were total opposites.

"Why don't you two play a game of catch?" Princess Alcmene said. She tossed her son a ball and went back into the palace.

"Catch, Eury!" called Hercules. He threw it. Eury missed it.

"Wild throw!" Eury wiped his nose with the back of his hand. "Go get the ball."

"No problem," said Hercules. He went after it.

Eury was a creepy little kid. But Hercules was being nice to him. I thought maybe he'd outgrown his bad temper. Wrong!

"Catch!" called Hercules. Once more he threw the ball to his cousin.

It was an easy little blooper of a throw. But Eury missed it.

"Wild throw! Wild throw!" whined Eury. "Get the ball yourself."

"Okay," said Hercules, and he did.

"I'm ready," called Eury. "Ready for someone else to play catch with!"

"I'll aim it better this time!" said Hercules. He threw the ball.

BONK!

It hit Eury right between the eyes.

"Oops!" said Hercules.

"Aunt Alcmene!" Eury cried, running toward

the palace. His nose was running like crazy. "Hercules hit me with the ball!"

"It was an accident," said Hercules when his mother rushed outside. "I was trying to throw it so he could catch it." He turned to his cousin. "Sorry, Eury."

"He did it on purpose!" Eury told Princess Alcmene.

"Did not," said Hercules.

I believed him.

But his mother wasn't so sure.

"All right, Hercules," she said. "You get a time-out."

Hercules had to sit on a stump for fifteen minutes and watch while his mom played catch with his slimy cousin.

When his time-out was over, Hercules got the ball back.

"Play nicely!" Princess Alcmene said, and she went back inside.

"Catch!" said Hercules. He threw a gentle, underhand toss.

Eury missed again.

"You can't throw the ball!" chanted Eury. "You can't throw at all!"

Hercules's eyes began to flash with anger. His face turned red.

I thought about whipping off my helmet and trying to calm him down. But to tell you the truth, I was half ready for Hercules to get back at that little stinker.

"I'm not chasing that ball," said Eury. "If you want it, go get it."

Hercules ran and picked up the ball. "Heads up!" he called, and he threw it.

BONK!

The ball hit Eury on the top of his head and bounced off.

"Ow!" cried Eury.

Hercules caught the ball in the air and threw it again.

BONK!

"Ow! OW!" cried Eury.

And again.

BONK!

"Auntieeeeee!" cried Eury.

When Eury's mother came to pick him up, she was horrified. "Eurystheus!" she cried. "Your little head! It's . . . it's all lumpy!"

Eury wiped his nose on his sleeve and pointed at Hercules. "He did it!"

"Beast!" Eury's mother yelled at Hercules.

"Hercules is sorry," said Princess Alcmene. "He wants to apologize!"

But Eury's mother dragged Eury off. Later, I heard that she spread the word to all the other moms in Thebes. She told them not to let their kids play with Hercules. That he was out of control.

After that, I didn't see Hercules for a while. No reason, really. I was busy in the Underworld. Then one day an invitation came:

Hercules is turning X!
Please come to his surprise birthday party
Next Saturday at X1:00

On the day of the party, I showed up. I'd brought the kid a great present — a complete set of Immortals of Wrestling cards. Very rare. Worth a fortune.

"Welcome, Hades!" said Princess Alcmene. "You're the first to arrive. We've invited every boy and girl in Thebes to come, too. They'll be here any minute."

"Is Eury coming?" I asked.

"No, he and his mom moved to Mycenae," said the princess. "But there will be lots and lots of kids."

But an hour later, only a two-year-old boy had shown up, little Theseus. His mother had brought him all the way from Troezen, which was why she hadn't heard about Hercules's temper.

When Hercules came into the nearly empty palace yard, he wasn't disappointed because he didn't know about the party. He was just happy to have such an enormous birthday cake all for himself and Theseus, who was too little to eat very much.

"This is a wake-up call, Alcmene," said Amphitryon after Theseus had gone home and the "party" was over. "We have to do something about Hercules," said Amphitryon. "His terrible temper has made him an outcast."

"The boy doesn't know his own strength," Alcmene admitted. "He could hurt someone someday." She turned to me. "You're his uncle, Hades. Can he come and stay with you for a while?"

"I'd like to help you out with this, Alcmene," I told her. "Really, I would. But live mortals aren't allowed down in the Underworld. Sorry."

"My second cousin Humus and his wife, Pita, have a dairy farm out in the middle of nowhere," Amphitryon said. "Why don't we send Hercules there? Cows are peaceful, mellow creatures. Maybe if he tends cows for a while, Hercules will mellow, too."

"All right," said Alcmene. "But you have to tell him."

"No, you," said Amphitryon.

In the end, they decided to write Hercules a note.

Dear Son,

Pack your bags! First thing tomorrow, you are leaving on a surprise adventure!

Your loving parents

P.S. Pack everything. You may be gone for a while.

Chapter V
NOT-SO-BIG ADVENTURE

I felt bad for Hercules, being banished and all. So I put on my helmet and stuck around — just in case he needed me.

That night, Hercules brushed his teeth, as usual. He put on his PJs. He was climbing into bed when he spied the note. He picked it up and began sounding out the words.

"Awesome!" he said when he'd read the whole thing and looked at the map Amphitryon had drawn on the back.

Right away, he started packing. He didn't wait for morning, but set off in the moonlight, following the map. I set off with him, though he didn't know it at the time.

Hercules walked for three whole nights and

three whole days. Even though he was only ten, he was bigger then most men. And many times stronger. So he felt completely safe out on his own.

On the morning of the fourth day, Hercules came to a farm. It was out in the middle of nowhere, just as Amphitryon had said.

"Whoa!" said Hercules. He looked very surprised. Was *this* where he was supposed to have an adventure? He knocked at the farmhouse door.

"You must be Hercules," said his stepfather's second cousin, when he opened it. "Welcome! You look like a good worker. Let's get you started, shall we?"

"Let him eat breakfast first, Humus," said his wife.

"Have it your way, Pita," said Humus.

Humus and Pita laid out a huge spread of dairy products from their cows: cottage cheese, cream cheese, yogurt, and butter. Hercules ate a big breakfast. I managed to snag a piece of cheese for myself. I sprinkled on some of my Ambro-Salt, and it wasn't half bad. When Hercules was finished eating, Humus and Pita walked him out to the barn.

Hercules patted the first big black-and-white cow he came to. "Nice cow," he said. "Can I take care of this one?"

"You get to take care of the whole herd," said Humus.

Hercules looked down on the row of stalls. There were hundreds of cows. Hercules smiled. "No problem!"

I stuck around for a couple of weeks. I waited until Hercules got into a routine. Each morning, he fed the cows hay. Then he led them to the pasture to graze. While the cows were grazing, Hercules mucked out the barn. This was no small task, as it was a huge barn with lots and lots of muck.

In the evening, Hercules put out fresh hay for the cows. He filled their troughs with fresh water. After that, he went to the pasture and led his cows back to the barn for the night. He sat with them until they fell asleep. Then Hercules climbed into his own bed, which was in the barn, and fell asleep, too.

Life on the farm wasn't much of a surprise adventure. But Hercules liked the cows. He never complained.

Princess Alcmene and Amphitryon never told anyone where Hercules was going. Not that anyone asked. Everyone seemed just as happy to have him out of the way. I figured Hera would have a hard time finding out where he was. I felt the boy was safe out on the farm, so I took off.

Hercules stayed on the farm and took care of the cattle for eight years. I checked on him from time to time. Humus and Pita grew fat and lazy, letting Hercules do all the work. But Hercules grew stronger and stronger.

One day when I stopped by to check on Hercules, Pita had just handed him a letter that had come for him. I read it over his shoulder:

Dear Hercules,

Happy birthday, Son! You are eighteen today. We'll bet your little temper problems are a thing of the past.

Now the time has come for you to decide what path you will follow when you go out into the world. Stop by the palace and see us sometime!

Your loving parents

Hercules scratched his head. "What do they mean 'go out into the world'?"

"That's what they said?" asked Pita, alarmed.

"They don't mean it!" said Humus. "Forget going out into the world!"

"Stay here, Hercules," said Pita. "You can have all the yogurt you want."

Hercules nodded. But I could tell he was puzzled. I followed invisibly behind him as he headed out to the pasture. He sat down among the cows. He pulled up a handful of grass and chewed on it while he thought.

I was just about to take off my helmet and have a chat with Hercules when I saw two tall women walking toward him. Ye gods! Where had they come from? I decided to stay invisible.

Hercules saw them, too. He blinked. His mouth gaped open in surprise.

The women stopped before him. Both were very beautiful. One wore a plain white robe. The other wore a fancy red robe with way too much gold trim.

"Greetings, Hercules!" said the one in the red-and-gold robe.

Hercules almost choked on his grass. "How do you know my name?"

"We know all about you," said the white-robed woman. "You are trying to choose which path in life to follow."

"Whoa!" exclaimed Hercules. "You *do* know everything. Can you help me?"

"That's why we're here." The white robed woman smiled.

Who were these two? I'd never seen them before. Neither had a goddess glow. But they didn't look like mortals, either. I didn't trust them.

"Follow my path, Hercules," said the red-robed woman. "You will always eat good food and drink fine wine. You will have servants. You will never have to work hard. You will have piles and piles of gold. What fun you shall have!"

"Fun!" said Hercules. "Whoa!"

"Follow my path, Hercules," said the white-robed woman. "On this path, you will help those who cannot help themselves. You will do back-breaking labor. You will work and sweat and toil. Then you will work and sweat and toil some more. Horrible monsters will try to kill you. You will almost always be in terrible danger. But the gods will respect you."

"Respect," said Hercules. "Whoa!"

"You must choose, Hercules," said the red-robed woman.

"Which path will you follow?" said the one in white.

"Let me think," said Hercules. He didn't say anything for the longest time. The two women looked at each other.

"We thought this might happen," said the white-robed woman.

"So we each wrote a list for you," said the red-robed woman.

They handed their lists to Hercules. Here's what they said:

EASY PATH	HARD PATH
NO HARD WORK	BACK-BREAKING LABOR
GOOD MEATS AND CHEESES	GRUEL, BREAD CRUSTS, ETC.
FINE WINES	WATER, IF YOU CAN FIND IT
SERVANTS	HORRIBLE MONSTERS
PILES OF GOLD	THANKS FROM THE HELPLESS
FUN!	CONSTANT DANGER

Hercules sounded out the words on the lists. Then he smiled. "It's a no-brainer," he said. "I choose the hard path."

"You're kidding!" said both women at the same time. "Why?"

"All I've had to eat for the past VIII years is cheese," said Hercules. "I can't take any more."

I slapped my invisible forehead with my invisible hand. Hercules was letting *cheese* determine his fate?

"Is that your final answer?" asked the white-robed woman.

Hercules nodded.

The white-robed woman burst out laughing. "I won! I won!"

"Oh, don't rub it in," said the red-robed woman. She glared at Hercules. "Are you ever going to be sorry!"

"Come on!" said the white-robed woman. "Let's go tell Hera!"

Hera! Had she sent these women?

I jumped to my feet, but I was too late.

POOF! The women vanished into thin air.

CHAPTER VI
BIG FOOT

"Strange," Hercules muttered to himself as he got to his feet. "But at least now I know which path to follow. All I have to do is find out where it starts."

He headed back down the hill. I ran invisibly behind him. When he reached the farm, he found Humus and Pita running around, very upset.

"Whoa!" said Hercules. "What's wrong?"

"A huge lion is on the mountain!" said Humus.

"He will come down tonight and eat our cows!" said Pita. "And there is nothing we can do to stop him!"

"Is, too!" Hercules cried. His eyes flashed with

anger. "I'll save the cows! I'll slay this evil lion! I'll bash him to bits!"

All those years hanging out with the mellow cows hadn't mellowed Hercules at all. One lion shows up and *bam!* He's ready to bash heads.

Hercules ran over to a tree. He broke off a huge limb.

"I have a club, lion!" he shouted. "And here I come to bash you with it!" He raced up the mountain.

"Come back, Hercules!" Pita shouted after him. "This lion is a horrible monster!"

"A horrible monster?" said Hercules. "Good! That means I am on the right path!"

Hercules kept running. I ran after him. Halfway up the mountain some big footprints appeared in the path. Hercules stopped.

"Your big feet don't scare me, lion!" he bellowed.

He was answered by a bone-rattling roar.

The roar only made Hercules run faster. He followed those lion tracks all the way to the top of the mountain. I followed him. Keeping up with Hercules was exhausting, even for a god. At last, just as the sun was setting, Hercules came upon the lion. From the sound of his roar, I'd expected a majestic beast. But this was a scrawny specimen. He lay stretched out on a boulder, snoozing.

The lion heard Hercules coming and looked up, smothering a yawn.

"You're not going to eat my cows, lion!" Hercules growled.

"You got that right," said the lion, sitting up. "I'm a vegetarian."

"A *what*?" said Hercules.

"I eat vegetables," the lion explained. "Fruit, seeds, nuts. A little fish. But no red meat. Doesn't agree with me. I'm not after your cows. The name's Cithaeron, by the way, but everyone calls me Cee. And you are . . . ?"

"I am what?" said Hercules.

"I mean, what's your name?" said the lion.

"Hercules," our hero answered. He lowered his club. But he still looked suspicious. "How come I can understand the speech of a lion?"

"Long ago, I ate a little wood nymph," said Cee. "Didn't mean to do it. I was eating a fig leaf, and she was on it. Ever since, I've had the gift of speech."

"Why were you roaring?" Hercules asked.

"That wasn't me," said Cee. "That was my cousin, NeMean. He's the meanest lion ever. And he *is* after your cows."

Another thunderous roar split the air.

Hercules waved his club over his head. "You'll never get my cows, NeMean!" he shouted. "I'm coming to slay you!"

"Not with that tree branch, you won't," said Cee.

"It's a club," said Hercules. "And what's wrong with it?"

"Nothing," said Cee. "But NeMean has impenetrable skin."

"Oh," said Hercules. "I had a rash once. Itched like crazy."

"*Impenetrable* means no weapon can hurt him," said Cee. "No weapon can pierce his skin."

"What about a sword?" asked Hercules.

"Nope."

"Bow and arrow?"

Cee shook his head.

"Spear?" said Hercules.

"Not even."

"Battle-axe?"

"Listen," said Cee, "you can stand here and name weapons all night long. But not one of them can kill NeMean."

"Then I'll go after him with my bare hands!" growled Hercules.

"That could work," said Cee. "But you might get hurt. I have a better idea."

"What?" said Hercules.

"NeMean fears only one thing in this world," said Cee. "Lester the Lion Slayer."

"Never heard of him," said Hercules.

"Lester slew NeMean's grandfather," said Cee. "He skinned him and flung the skin over his shoulders as a cape. Then Lester hollowed out his head and set it on his own head as a helmet. Now he looks out at the world through the lion's great jaws. Revolting, huh?"

"Awesome," said Hercules. He looked off into the night sky, as if picturing himself wearing just this sort of getup.

"What if NeMean thought you were Lester?" said Cee.

"Do I look like Lester?" asked Hercules.

"No," said Cee. "But you might if you had on a lion cape and helmet."

Hercules nodded. "Well, so long, pal." He raised his club over Cee's head.

"Hold it! Hold it!" shouted Cee. "You don't have to kill me!"

Hercules looked suspicious. "How else can I get a lion cape?"

"I can drape myself around your shoulders like a cape," said Cee. "Then I'll rest my head on top of yours. Up close, it wouldn't look that believable. But from a distance, it should be good enough to scare NeMean away and save your cattle."

"And my cows, too?" said Hercules.

"Er, yes," said Cee. "Your cows, too."

Hercules hesitated for a moment. "If you're

NeMean's cousin," he said at last, "why aren't you on his side?"

"You like all *your* cousins?" asked Cee.

Hercules wrinkled his nose. I could tell he was thinking of Eury. He shook his head.

"Well, I don't like NeMean," said Cee. "He stole me away from my mama when I was a little baby lion. He makes me wait on him. He thinks I'll try to make a break for it when he goes off hunting, so . . . " Cee held up his left hind foot. A chain was looped around his ankle. Attached to the other end of the chain was a great big rock.

Hercules bent down, grabbed the chain with both hands, and began to pull. His muscles bulged out bigger and bigger and then — *SNAP!*

"Wow, thanks!" Cee rubbed the spot where the chain had been.

"No problem." Hercules turned his back to the lion and bent down. "Hop on."

Cee jumped onto Hercules's back. He threw his front legs over one side of his neck. He swung his back legs over the other. He rested his chin on top of Hercules's head.

"Giddy-up, horsie!" said Cee.

"What?" said Hercules.

"Never mind," said Cee. "Let's go save your cows."

Hercules ran back down the mountain with the lion on his shoulders. Naturally, I ran behind. The cows were snoozing peacefully in the field. NeMean had yet to strike. Hercules slipped inside the barn. I did, too. Hercules peeked out from a crack in the door. I did the same.

There, in the moonlight, I saw the silhouette of a giant lion. What a monster! I had no idea lions could grow *that* big. NeMean was crouched behind an olive tree. Slowly, slowly, he crept toward the cows. He began moving faster and faster, until he was racing for the herd. Another half minute and he'd be upon them!

"Go!" said Cee. "Now! Before it's too late!"

"But what do I say?" said Hercules.

"Say you're Lester!" said Cee.

Hercules leapt out of the barn and shouted, "You're Lester!"

NeMean skidded to a stop, leaving a trail of

claw marks in the dirt. In the moonlight, I saw his eyes open wide.

"Now what?" whispered Hercules.

"Say your old lion cape is worn out," whispered Cee. "Say you're looking for a new one."

"Your cape is old!" shouted Hercules. "You're looking for a new one!"

It made no sense, but evidently the mere mention of Lester's name was powerful enough to scare NeMean half to death. The giant lion spun around and started running up the mountain. He kept looking back over his shoulder, and suddenly *BAM!* He rammed into a tree trunk and fell to the ground.

"Whoa!" said Hercules. "That's gotta hurt!"

"I never meant for *this* to happen," said Cee. "I wonder if he's . . ."

Cee jumped off Hercules's shoulders. The two ran to where the giant lion lay. Cee picked up his forepaw and felt for his pulse. Then he sadly shook his head. Considering how mean NeMean had been, Cee was very forgiving.

"Um, do you think I could maybe have his impossible . . . im . . . whatever . . . skin?" asked Hercules. "That no-weapon-can-pierce thing is awesome."

"Yes, take it," said Cee. "NeMean would like that."

It didn't take Hercules long to fashion a breast plate and helmet out of NeMean.

"He looks great on you," said Cee.

Humus and Pita had watched all this happen. Their eyes were filled with wonder. Then their eyes filled with tears, because it was pretty clear that Hercules wasn't going to stick around the cattle farm much longer. He was ready to leave and take up his life as a hero. And when he left, Humus and Pita would have to go back to mucking out the cattle barn themselves.

CHAPTER VII
BIG JOB

"Mmmmmmooooooo moo moo!" said Hercules. "Bye, cows!"

After all those years with the cattle, Hercules had learned to speak Cow.

"Mooo maaa. Moooo," he added. "I'll come back and see you."

"Will you be back often?" asked Humus, sounding hopeful. "We could save the mucking for you."

"Oh, let the boy go," said Pita. "Can't you see he's fated for bigger things than mucking?"

In fact, Hercules was not done with mucking. But I'm getting ahead of the story.

After Hercules said his goodbyes, he turned to the lion. "Hop on," he said.

"You're wearing NeMean now," said Cee. "You don't need me."

"He makes a good hat and breastplate," said Hercules. "But you keep my neck warm."

Cee took his place on Hercules's shoulders, and our hero set off down the road.

I thought Hercules and Cee made a pretty good team. I figured that with Hercules's strength and Cee's good-hearted sense they'd be all right on their own. But before I went back to the Underworld, I wanted to wish Hercules good luck.

"Hercules," I said. "It's me, Hades." I took off my helmet. *FOOP!* I appeared beside him.

"Yikes!" said Cee.

"Hey, Uncle Hades!" Hercules grinned.

"Hades?" said Cee. "As in Lord Hades? Ruler of the Underworld?"

"The one and only," I confessed.

"Oh, this is a *major* thrill!" said Cee.

I liked him right away.

"Uncle Hades," said Hercules, "you should have seen what just happened."

"Actually, I did." I told him how I'd been

invisibly there. "I have to get back to the Underworld, but I wanted to wish you luck first. Where are you going? What's your plan?"

Hercules turned to the lion. "Do we have a plan, Cee?"

"Of course," said the lion. "First we're going to walk to the oracle of Delphi. I'm going to ask the sibyl what to do with myself, since I'm not NeMean's prisoner anymore."

I nodded and turned to Hercules. "And what will you ask the sibyl?"

He wrinkled his brow in thought. "Where the path is," he said at last. "You know, the hard path?"

"Good idea," I told him. "Well, good luck on your journey, both of you. And Hercules, be careful. You know Hera is still out to get you."

"I can take her," said Hercules, putting his fists together and popping out his biceps.

"She's a powerful goddess with a grudge," I reminded him. "It's not about muscles."

"Right," said Hercules. "Don't worry about me!"

But that was the thing. I *did* worry. I went back to the Underworld. I attended the opening of a wrestling stadium in my kingdom, which was a minor disaster. And I even helped Theseus out of a few jams. But I could never get my mind off Hercules. He was big. But up against Hera, he was helpless. So, when I got the chance, I astro-traveled straight to Mount Parnassus, home to the oracle of Delphi. *ZIP!* My timing couldn't have been better. Hercules and Cee had just gone into the sibyl's cave. Invisible, I let myself in, too — saving the ridiculous $XV admission price.

The sibyl was always a lovely young mortal priestess. She always wore a white robe. That day the sibyl had on a white robe. But she had a mop of long, tangled hair that hid her face completely. Being a sibyl is a demanding job. I doubted that sibyls had much free time to devote to hair care. Still, this sibyl's hair was an unruly mess. A rat's nest! She could have run a comb through it, at the very least. You'd think an oracle as famous as the one at Delphi would have *some* standards.

As always, the sibyl sat on a tall three-legged stool called a "tripod."

"Speak, pilgrim!" said the sibyl as Hercules and Cee approached. "What is your question for the oracle?"

That voice. It was so familiar. I wondered if I'd spoken to this sibyl before she let herself go in the hair department.

"You go," Hercules told Cee.

Cee slipped off Hercules's shoulders and cleared his throat. "I am Cithaeron, a lion," he said.

"The point!" snapped the sibyl. "Get to it."

"I'd like to know what to do with my life," said Cee. "Can you tell me?"

The ratty-haired sibyl leaned waaaaaay over the steep precipice. She took a deep breath of the thick yellow smoke that billowed up from way down inside the earth. I feared that any second her stool was going to tip too far and send her crashing down to whatever lay below.

"The lion wishes to know what to do with his life!" the sibyl shouted into the abyss.

Clouds of yellow smoke billowed up. For a moment, they hid the sibyl entirely. When the smoke cleared, the sibyl leaned back so that all three legs of her tripod were on the ground. That was a relief.

"Hear me, lion," the sibyl said. "Like honey dripping from the beehive, so shall you live."

"*What?*" said Cee. "What does *that* mean?"

But the sibyl only said, "Next pilgrim!"

"I can't believe this," muttered Cee as he stepped back.

Hercules stepped forward. "Where does the hard path begin?" he asked.

Again, the sibyl leaned precariously over the yellow smoke. When she brought her stool back to an upright position, she said, "The hard path begins at King Eurystheus's palace in Mycenae."

Hercules stared at the sibyl in disbelief. "You mean my cousin, Eury? He's a king now?"

The sibyl nodded. "You must go to his palace. You must kneel down before King Eurystheus. He will give you —"

"No way!" Hercules's eyes flashed with anger.

Even in the dim light of the cave, I saw that his face was turning red. "I'm not kneeling down before that tattletale!"

"Never interrupt a sibyl!" warned the sibyl.

"Sorry," murmured Hercules.

"King Eurystheus will give you XII labors to do, Hercules," the sibyl continued. "XII hard labors. Some — most, really — are impossible."

That voice. I still couldn't place it. And I'd never heard such a talkative sibyl.

"Hard labors?" Hercules was saying. "No problem. Impossible labors? Bring 'em on. But I won't do them for Eury."

"You must!" said the sibyl. "That is your fate. Now, get to work, Hercules!" She bowed her shaggy head. "Next pilgrim!"

Puzzled, I followed Cee and Hercules out of the cave. Sibyls often gave strange, hard-to-figure-out messages, like the one about the dripping honey that she gave to poor Cee. But this sibyl had straight-out told Hercules what to do. Something was wrong here, and it wasn't just the sibyl's nasty hairdo.

"Very strange," Cee was saying. "All I can figure is that honey is sticky, so I guess I'll stick with you for a while, Hercules."

"Right," said Hercules. "Hop on!"

I let them go ahead. I turned around and snuck back into the cave. And when I saw what was going on, I almost fell over the precipice myself.

There stood a lovely young mortal woman in a white robe. A sibyl. She was helping the ratty-haired sibyl off the high stool.

"And did you enjoy playing a funny trick on your friend?" asked the lovely sibyl.

"I did indeed," said the second sibyl. Then she reached up and took off what turned out to be a wig of long, snarled hair. "I did indeed."

It was Hera!

CHAPTER VIII
BIG MOUTH

Hera! No wonder her voice had sounded familiar. What a sneak! She was a Power Olympian, and she'd talked an innocent sibyl into trading places with her so she could play a "funny trick." Funny to her, maybe. Now I knew that every one of the XII labors would be designed to get rid of Hercules.

After their visit to the sibyl, Hercules and Cee started off for Mycenae. I ducked back down to the Underworld. When I got there, I was surprised to find my queen, Persephone, waiting for me in the den.

"Hades, where have you been?" she asked.

"On earth," I told her. "Checking on Hercules. Didn't you get my note?"

"I got it, Hades," Persephone said. "You know, I've hardly seen you this winter. It's the only time we get to spend together. I guess I was hoping you'd stay home."

"Oh, Phoney, honey," I said. "I want that, too. But Hercules is in real trouble." I told her about Hera impersonating the sibyl and sending Hercules off to do XII labors for Eury. "If I don't go up to earth to help him, there's no telling what might happen to him."

"I'll bet you'd be surprised by what he can do on his own," said Persephone.

I shook my head. "No, he needs me, P-phone," I said. "He's our nephew, after all. And he's a mortal. Any one of these XII labors could be the end of him. That's what Hera's hoping."

"Have it your way, Hades," said my queenie. "Winter's almost over, anyway. Then I'll be gone for nine months. You think you could help Hercules finish up all his labors by the time I come home next winter?"

"Count on it," I told her. "Next winter it's you and me, sitting by the fire."

"Plus a few dinners at the Underworld Grill?" Persephone smiled hopefully.

"Deal," I said to her.

I went back up to earth the next day. I arrived in time to see Hercules walk through the city gates of Mycenae. Cee was still on his shoulders. I hiked invisibly along up the steep hill to King Eurystheus's palace, which stood on a mountaintop. A huge bronze pot sat beside the palace door. It had no lid. It was too big to be of any real use. What was it for, I wondered?

Hercules pounded on the palace door.

A frightened-looking servant opened it. "Come in," he said, looking over his shoulder. "King Eurystheus is sitting on his throne, waiting to see you."

"Hercules will not set foot inside this palace," Cee told the servant. "If the king wants to see him, let him come to the door himself."

The servant's eyes popped open in surprise. Clearly not many people — and even fewer lions — gave orders to the king. But he scurried away. A few minutes later, King Eury appeared at the door. A big gold crown sat on his surprisingly small head.

Eury had grown tall. But under his oversized crown, I could tell he was the same runny-nosed bully who had taunted Hercules all those years before.

When he saw Hercules standing before him, nearly as big as a god and wearing a lion's-head helmet, King Eury shrank back into the palace. He all but shut the door, leaving only a little crack. "It's good that you didn't come inside and smell up my palace," King Eury said from behind the door.

"You are to give Hercules XII labors," Cee told the king. "So give."

King Eury opened the door halfway. "Don't tell me what to do!" He wiped his nose on his silken sleeve. In his hand, he held a slip of parchment. "Here's the deal. Either you'll rid the earth of twelve horrible, monstrous things and make me look good — or one of the twelve monstrous things will get rid of you." Eury smiled, showing a mouth full of crooked yellow teeth. "I'll read you the first one." He looked down at the parchment.

"Labor I: Slay the monster lion, NeMean, who eats everyone's cattle, and bring me his impenetrable pelt."

Hercules brightened. "Check!"

King Eury frowned. "What does that mean?"

"It means check it off the list," said Hercules. "I'm wearing NeMean." He took off his lion helmet and breastplate. He held them out to Eury. "Here."

"Just put them on the stoop," said King Eury, not wanting to risk opening the door wider.

"All right!" said Hercules. "One down and only . . . " He wrinkled his forehead and began counting on his fingers.

"Eleven to go," Cee whispered.

"Here's a little background on your next labor," said King Eury. "A terrible Hydra monster lives in a swamp in Lerna. It has nine disgusting heads. When it breathes its poisonous breath on goats, cattle, sheep, shepherds, whatever, they drop dead. So, here's Labor II: Go to Lerna, slay the Hydra, and bring it to me!" The king laughed. "See you — never!" He slammed the door.

I groaned. Long ago, when I was chasing the monster Typhon, I'd gone to his foul-smelling cave in Sicily and found his wife, Echidna, with their brood of monstrous children. One of them was my own three-headed guard dog, Cerberus. There was also the goat-headed Chimera. And the riddle-telling Sphinx, part-lion, part-girl. Hydra was another of Echidna's offspring. I remembered her as a nine-headed freak who gave new meaning to the term "bad breath." But still, she *was* Cerbie's sister. Cerbie was family to me. And that made Hydra — well, some sort of way-distant cousin. I couldn't let Hercules slay her. I thought I'd better go and have a talk with Hydra's mom.

I knew it would take Hercules and Cee a few days to get to Lerna. While they were on their way, I astro-traveled to Sicily.

ZIP!

I landed just outside the mouth of Typhon and Echidna's cave.

"Hello? Echidna?" I called. "Hades here. Anybody home?"

"Hades?" answered a musical voice. "Come in!"

I made my way into the cave. The last time I'd been there, it was a dark, dank monsters' lair. But now, to my surprise, the place was light and airy. It had been totally redone, with Italian-tile floors and walls painted in muted pastels.

Echidna was sitting behind a desk. Well, "sitting" isn't exactly the word, since her bottom half was that of a huge speckled serpent. Echidna was more *coiled* behind the desk. Her top half, that of a beautiful woman, was dressed in a neat white robe.

"Surprised, Hades?" Echidna said. "Hey, it's just me now. The kids are all grown and out on their own. My husband lives under a mountain."

"Hmmm, sorry about that," I mumbled. I hoped she didn't hold it against me that I'd sent Mount Etna tumbling on top of Typhon.

"Don't apologize, Hades," said Echidna. "I've never been happier. I'll make us some tea." She got up and slithered over to a state-of-the-art kitchen. "So, how do you like the cave?"

"It looks fantastic," I told her. "It should be in one of those home-decorating magazines."

"You think?" Echidna smiled. "I did it myself. Typhon would never let me fix up the place. He thought *Architectural Digest* was what you did after you ate somebody's house. But now I've started my own decorating business." I sat down at a table. Echidna poured our tea. "I did Sphinx's new place over in Egypt. Surrounded it with lots of big stone pyramids. Very dramatic."

"Speaking of your kids," I said, "I came to talk to you about one of them."

Echidna's smile faded. "Cerberus? Is he all right?"

"He's fine," I said. "Excellent guard dog. No, it's Hydra."

"Oh, poor Hydra!" Echidna sighed. "When she was a little nine-headed baby monster, her breath stank. But when she got older, it turned poisonous. Very strong stuff. One little 'Hello!' can kill an army. So I sent her to live in a deserted, foul-smelling swamp in Lerna where she can't do much harm. I figured the swamp smelled so bad already that her breath couldn't make much difference. Hydra's got problems, but she's not a bad girl. She always obeys her mother, I'll say that for her. Well, what's she done now?"

"It's not what she's done," I said. "It's what someone wants done to her." I explained about King Eurystheus and how he'd told Hercules to kill Hydra.

Echidna only laughed. "Hercules can't kill her," she said. "One of Hydra's heads — the one with the big mouth — is immortal. Oh, and if there is a battle, be sure to tell Hercules not to cut off Hydra's other heads, either. If he does, two heads will sprout up in the place of every one he chops off."

"I hope there won't be any battle," I said.

"Monsters and heroes are fated to battle." Echidna shrugged. "You know, Hades, Hydra has a hard life in that dreary swamp. The world is always unkind when you've got really, really bad breath. And Hydra's is the worst." She shook her head. "Be sure to give her my love when you see her. And if you want her to do something, just tell her I said so."

"Thanks, Echidna." I invited her to come down and visit Cerberus some time. She said she would and even offered to help Persephone and me if we ever decided to redo Villa Pluto.

I left Echidna's cave, put on my Helmet of Darkness, and chanted the astro-traveling spell for Lerna.

ZIP!

And P.U.!

I found myself standing ankle deep in smelly swamp ooze. Not three dekafeet from me, a battle was already underway. Hercules held a huge wooden club. Cee was yelling directions to him. Both were covered head to toe in swamp goo.

Cee pointed to a wide circle of bubbles coming up from beneath the thick brown water.

"Here she comes!" shouted the lion.

And up from the swamp sprang Hydra. Her monstrous body was no more than a blob. From it sprouted nine long snaky stalks. Each stalk was topped with at least one small head, no bigger than a fist. Each little fist of a head had a human face.

"Get that head, Hercules!" shouted Cee, pointing.

Hercules drew back his club and took a mighty swing.

THWACK!

The little head went flying.

PLOP! It landed in the swamp.

Instantly, two more little heads popped out of the end of the stalk.

Hydra had more than nine heads now. Many more! I figured the battle must have been raging for some time. If ever a hero needed help, it was Hercules.

I whipped off my helmet and tossed it into my wallet. "Stop fighting!" I called, making the classic time-out T with my hands. "Hydra! Hercules! Cee! Hold it!"

The three stopped thrashing and splashing through the swamp.

"Whoa!" said Hercules. "Back off, Hades. I was about to slay the Hydra!"

"I don't think so," I said.

"I don't think so either," muttered Cee.

I turned to face the monster. "Hydra," I said. "I am Hades, King of the Underworld."

One of Hydra's head stalks thrust itself up above the others. Two little eyes met mine. Then Hydra opened her jaws wider and wider until the little head was all mouth.

"Hhhhhhello, Hhhhhhades," she said.

CHAPTER IX
BIG POT

Hydra's breath hit me like a hammer. I'm immortal. It couldn't kill me. But it made me horribly sick to my stomach.

"Dive!" I managed to call to Hercules and Cee.

They dove under the swampy waters. I drew a deep godly breath and blew Hydra's poisoned greeting far away. By the time Hercules and Cee popped up again, the air was breathable.

"Don't talk," I told Hydra. "Listen."

Hydra's big mouth slowly closed. She tilted her head, ready to hear what I had to say.

"I was just visiting your mother in her cave," I said. "She sends you her love."

Hydra's big mouth curved up in a smile.

"Hercules doesn't really want to fight you," I said.

"Do, too," Hercules muttered under his breath.

"But he must do XII labors." I quickly explained how Hera and King Eurystheus were out to get Hercules. "Your mother would like you to help Hercules, Hydra. If you're willing to help him, nod."

Hydra eagerly nodded all of her heads.

"Good," I said. "Then you must go to Mycenae with Hercules and Cee. You must let them present you to King Eury."

Hydra's heads started nodding again.

"I'm sure the king won't want to keep you around," I said. "So after he checks you off the list, you'll be free to come back here. Or go wherever you please." I frowned. "Except for your, uh, little breath problem."

Hydra hung her heads in shame.

"Hydra?" said Cee. "Is it true that you've been terrifying the neighborhood? And poisoning every mortal man, woman, or beast who comes near the swamp?"

Hydra shrugged her little blob-like shoulders.

"You didn't mean to?" asked Cee.

Hydra shook her head vehemently.

"It was an accident, right?" Hercules asked. He knew all about accidents.

Hydra nodded. She seemed grateful that, at last, these two seemed to understand.

Now Hydra reached up with a surprisingly elegant pair of hands. She felt around on her head stalks. During the battle, multiple heads had sprouted on some of them. Now she began plucking off the extras. When picked, each one shriveled up, and she tossed what was left of it into the swamp. When she finished her weeding, she was her old nine-headed self again. All nine mouths smiled at us.

I thought Echidna would be pleased with the way this was turning out.

I walked with Hercules, Cee, and Hydra to the edge of the swamp. Hydra waded out of the water. She had extremely short legs. Her feet were big wide flippers. Walking to Mycenae with her was going to take a l-o-o-o-o-o-o-o-ng time.

"I can carry you," Hercules told Hydra. He reached out for her, but she bent her knees and sprang up, landing on top of his head. She gripped it with her flipper feet.

"Awesome," said Hercules. "Hop on!" he told Cee, and the lion took his usual place around our hero's neck.

"Have a good trip!" I called after the odd-looking trio as they set off down the road.

I dashed down to the Underworld for a few days, but I was back in time to see Hercules and company stride through the gates of Mycenae. I wore my helmet, though. This was Hercules's big moment. I didn't want the crowd to be distracted by the presence of a god.

The citizens of Mycenae gathered around Hercules. They stared at the big, muscular hero wearing a lion around his shoulders and the world's oddest head ornament. They ran toward the palace shouting, "Hercules is coming! Hercules is coming!"

By the time Hercules had reached the palace, a huge crowd had gathered.

"Eury!" Hercules called. He never could bring himself to call his cousin *King* Eury. "I'm back!"

There was no answer.

"Eury!" called Hercules. "I've brought Hydra."

"Hooray! Hooray!" shouted the crowd.

"Put it down on the stoop," came a disembodied voice.

"Eury?" Hercules looked around. "Are you inside that big bronze pot?"

"What if I am?" Eury's voice wafted up out of the opening. "A king has to protect himself so he can rule," he added. "I'm doing this for the good of my people."

Hercules broke into a grin. "Come out and get your Hydra."

A small slotted panel slid open about mid-pot. Eury's eyes peered out at us. "I see it," he said. "I'll check it off the list."

"Two down!" said Hercules. He reached up and slapped hands with Hydra. "Thanks, buddy!"

Hydra nodded. Then she jumped off Hercules's back. She waddled over to the big bronze pot.

Hydra came only halfway to the top of the pot. But as she stood there, her neck stalks began to extend up, up, up.

The crowd hushed. Everyone watched in amazement as Hydra's neck stalks kept on growing.

"What's happening out there?" called Eury. "Guards? This is your king speaking to you, guards. Tell me what's happening!"

Hydra's neck stalks reached the rim of the pot. Still they grew.

"Guards!" called Eury. "Guards? Can you hear me? Calling all guards! Get me out of here, or I'll fire the lot of you!"

Now Hydra bent her neck stems, and with all nine heads she peered over the rim of the pot to see the king in hiding.

"Guards! Obey me, now!" Eury called. "It's dark in here. "And I'm getting a cramp in my leg. Get over here, on the double. It's —"

That must have been when King Eury looked up. He let out an ichor-curdling scream:

"*AAAAAAAAAAAAAAAAAAAAAAAAA HHHHHHHHHHHHHHHHHHHHHHHHHHH!*"

And then we all heard a *CLUNK* as King Eury
fainted dead away inside his big bronze pot.

CHAPTER X
BIG KICK

It took dozens of palace guards, plus all the king's servants, to tip the big bronze pot over on its side. Two guards went into the pot, dragged out Eury, and carried him into the palace.

Hydra reached up a hand to cover her biggest mouth as she laughed. She didn't want to poison any bystanders.

"Look," said Cee, pointing to the pot. "There's a piece of parchment. King Eury must have dropped it when he fainted. I'll bet it tells what the next labor is."

Hercules ran over to get it. He handed it to Cee. "You read it."

"Labor III," Cee read. "Bring me the wild deer with antlers of gold and hooves of brass who has been trampling farmers' fields near Mount Ceryneia."

I'd heard about this deer. It was a hind — a female deer — but it had antlers, like a stag. It belonged to Artemis, goddess of the chase and the hunt.

Hydra insisted on going with Hercules and Cee to find the hind, and the three set off. I bid them goodbye, then astro-traveled to Artemis's earthly hunting lodge.

ZIP!

I found myself in a clearing in the woods. Hounds began barking and snarling. I'd managed to land beside a picnic table where Artemis was having a dinner for one.

Artemis leapt to her feet. Before I had a chance to open my mouth, she'd strung her bow and had an arrow pointed at my chest.

"Take it easy, Artemis!" I said. "It's me, Hades." Artemis had won the gold medal for archery in the first Olympics. I didn't want her taking a shot at me.

Artemis lowered her weapon. Her hounds

stopped snarling. "Why are you here?" Artemis asked. Then she looked hopeful. "You want to go hunting?"

"No, thanks," I said. "Don't let me interrupt your dinner. Sit! We can talk while you eat."

I sat down across from Artemis as she sank her teeth into a big meaty thighbone of some sort. And I told her why I'd come.

"Hercules would like to borrow your hind," I said. "Show it to King Eurystheus. Then he'll bring it right back to you."

Artemis rolled her eyes. "One doesn't go around borrowing deer as if they were library books or cups of sugar." She put two fingers into her mouth and gave an earsplitting whistle. Distant hoof beats sounded. In less than a minute, a majestic white deer appeared at the edge of the clearing. She walked straight to Artemis, her brass hooves gleaming. She bent her head, taking great care to keep her huge rack of golden antlers from doing any harm. Artemis gave her head a rub, then put an arm around her neck.

"Hello, Precious," she said. "Would you like to be borrowed?"

Precious shook her head, stomped a brass hoof, and gave a whuffle.

Sounded like "no" to me.

"Sorry, Hades," Artemis said. "Can't do it."

"I don't blame you," I told her. "Anyway, this is all Hera's doing."

"Hera?" Artemis's eyes darted around. "She didn't come with you, did she?"

"No, no," I said. "But she's the one who put King Eury up to this whole 'XII Labors of Hercules' thing. Don't worry about it, Artemis. It's not your problem." I stood to go.

"Wait, Hades." Artemis looked thoughtful. "I was hunting a wild boar the other day, and the beast ran by one of Hera's temples. I'm goddess of the chase, so naturally I chased after it. Hera happened to see me and stormed out of her temple, all bent out of shape. Now she's posted big NO HUNTING signs all over the place." She shook her head. "So, I think I'll help your friend after all, Hades. He can borrow Precious — if he can catch her."

She handed me the hind's golden collar.

"Once you slip this over her head, she will do what you say."

"Fair enough," I told her. "I'll tell Hercules."

Artemis gave Precious a pat on the flank, and the deer practically flew back into the woods. Hercules was a fast runner. But this hind was amazing. Catching her wasn't going to be easy.

I astro-traveled right back to Hercules. *ZIP!* He and his two companions were on their way to Mount Ceryneia. When they saw me, Hydra hopped off Hercules's head. Cee unwrapped himself from around his shoulders. The three sat down by the side of the road to rest. I sat down with them.

"I've got some good news," I told them. "And some bad news. First, the golden-antlered deer you're looking for belongs to Artemis. She calls her Precious and says you can borrow her to show to King Eury."

"All right!" said Hercules. "And what's the good news?"

"That *was* the good news," I said. "The bad

news is that you have to catch her first. And Precious can run like the wind."

"No problem!" Hercules jumped up. "Let's go."

I led the little party to the woods near Artemis's hunting lodge.

"Artemis whistled for Precious," I offered.

Hercules put his thumb and forefinger in his mouth and blew: *TWEEEEE!*

Now, Zeus's version of this labor in *The Big Fat Book of Greek Myths* says that Hercules chased after the golden-antlered hind for one whole year before catching her. Why T-BAMZ told this particular lie is anybody's guess. But here's what really happened.

No sooner had Hercules whistled than I caught a flash of golden antlers through the trees. Precious came to the edge of the clearing. She eyed Hercules warily.

"Maaaaa moooo," said Hercules. "Moooo oooom mooooo."

The deer's eyes flickered with understanding. Did Precious speak Cow? Or was Hercules speaking some sort of universal language understood by all big, hooved cud-chewers?

I never knew for sure, but whatever the case, Precious walked straight to Hercules. Our hero gave her a pat and slid the golden collar around her neck.

Precious was enormous, big enough to carry Hercules, Cee, and Hydra on her back all the way down one mountain and up another to King Eury's palace.

I met them there — *ZIP!* — just as the magnificent beast strode through the gates of Mycenae. As before, a crowd had gathered. The mortals had never seen such a wondrous animal as Precious, let alone one carrying a muscleman, a lion, and a strange, multi-headed monster. The crowd followed Precious, her brass hooves clacking on the road, all the way to the palace. They cheered and shouted, "Hooray for Hercules!"

"Eury!" called Hercules standing in front of the great pot. "Come out, and see the deer!"

The little slotted panel in the big bronze pot slid open. Eury's eye appeared.

"I see the antlers," King Eury's voice echoed from the pot. "Make the deer back up. I want to see its brass hooves."

"Show the king your brass hooves, Precious," said Hercules. "Mooooo maaa moo. Go on, show him!"

Precious whuffled in response. Then she showed him with a swift kick to the side of the pot. *BAM!*

"Ow!" cried Eury.

Precious kicked again. *BAM!*

And again. *BAM!*

It reminded me of the time little Hercules and little Eury had played catch.

"OW!" cried Eury again. He was so frightened he managed to leap out of the pot, all on his own, and run into the palace.

Minutes later a piece of parchment floated down from a palace window.

Cee picked it up and looked at it. "Uh-oh," he said.

CHAPTER XI

BIG BOAR

"Uh-oh?" said Hercules.

Cee nodded and read from the parchment: "Labor IV: Bring me the Boar of Erymanthus, who kills anyone unlucky enough to get near him." He shuddered. "I've heard of this boar. He's a heartless beast with gnarled tusks out to here." He extended a foreleg. "He eats muscle-bound heroes for breakfast."

"And I eat wild-boar sausage for lunch!" said Hercules. "Let's go get him!"

I offered to take Precious back to Artemis. I hopped onto her back, and off she galloped. It was an exciting ride but all too short. When we reached the hunting lodge, Precious stopped. I jumped down.

"Nice work, deer," I told her.

Precious gave me a whuffle and ran off into the woods. I was about to chant the astro-traveling spell and join up with Hercules when a terrible, ichor-chilling roar sounded. I'd only heard one roar like that before — it had come from the flaming mouth of the Calydonian Boar as he executed his famous Flying-Hoof Thrust that knocked my wrestling champ, Eagle-Eye Cyclops, flat on the mat.

A second savage roar sounded.

I didn't think it could be a Calydonian Boar. He ran Championship Wrestling School in Calydonia, teaching little piggy wrestling hopefuls all the right moves. But . . . could it be the Boar of Erymanthus? I headed into the woods to find out. I hadn't gone far when I came upon a pair of hairy wild boars. They were stomping the ground and roaring as they circled each other. Between them sat a pile of acorns. It looked as if the two boars were about to have a terrible fight over them.

If one of these beasts was the Boar of

Erymanthus, I didn't want him all bruised and beaten from a fight. No, I wanted him in tip-top shape so he could roar and stampede and scare the royal pants off Eury.

Quickly, I shifted my brain into CCC — Creature Communication Channel. It's a little power we gods have, and believe me it comes in handy when we want to talk to animals who don't have the gift of speech.

Boars! I thought. *Hold up a minute.*

The boars stopped circling.

What's he want? one boar thought to the other.

Search me, the second boar thought back. *Let's gore him.*

Hey, no, I come in peace, I thought to the boars. *I'm looking for the Wild Boar of Erymanthus.*

We're boars from Erymanthus, thought the first boar.

And we're pretty darned wild, thought the second.

This brought on a fit of snorting laughter.

Do you know the Boar of Erymanthus? I thought back. *I'd like to find him.*

Sure, we know him, thought the first boar. *But we're not telling you nothing!*

Never! thought the second boar. *Our lips are sealed!*

I'll gore him first, the first boar thought to the second. *Then you finish him off.*

Listen, I thought back. *I'm an immortal god. You can't kill me. I'll make you a deal. Tell me where I can find the Boar of Erymanthus, and I'll tell you where you can find the world's crunchiest acorns.*

He lives in Arcadia, the first boar thought quickly. *At the foot of Mount Erymanthus.*

He's big and pink, and he doesn't look dangerous, thought the second boar. *But he is. He's deadly.*

Now, where are the crunchy acorns? thought the first boar, drool dripping from his hairy lips.

In Dodona, I thought back. *It's that way.* I pointed.

The boars trotted off in the direction of Dodona, home to the sacred oaks of Zeus.

I chanted the astro-traveling spell for Mount Erymanthus. *ZIP!* I landed at the foot of the mountain. I blinked. And my godly heart nearly stopped. Hercules, Cee, and Hydra lay sprawled on the ground. What awful thing had happened? I ran over to them. Hydra was immortal. At least one of her heads had to be alive. But what about Hercules and Cee?

As I drew near, I heard a voice.

"And then I went over to this other tree," it said. "It had rough bark, so I leaned against it and gave my back a really good scratch. You think it's easy for a boar to scratch his own back? It is not."

I looked up. There, sitting on a stump, was a very large, very pink, and nearly hairless boar. He was doing the talking.

"Oh, sometimes I can get my brother to scratch my back," he was saying. "If he's not too busy, you know, rooting for acorns, things like that. He's got quite an appetite, my brother does, so he spends a lot of time rooting."

"Hello!" I said loudly, hoping to stop the flood of words.

The boar's black eyes flicked toward me. But he never stopped talking. "I didn't hear you coming," he said. "I have very good hearing as a rule. But you must have tippy-toed. We boars can't tippy-toe, because we don't have toes. We have hooves. I guess we could tippy-hoof, if we wanted to. But boars, as a rule, love to make a racket."

"Shhhh!" I said. "Quiet. You're the Boar of Erymanthus, aren't you?"

The big pink boar narrowed his beady eyes. "Good guess," he said. "Hardly anyone can tell. I don't look dangerous. I look like a nice pink piggy. And then — surprise! I can talk. Believe me, when a boar starts talking, everyone listens. And once they're listening. I never stop talking until everyone within hearing distance is a goner."

"So you . . . bore your victims to death?" I said.

The Wild Boar of Erymanthus nodded.

"I'll wake the others now," I told him. "And then, have we got a job for you."

"I don't generally take random jobs," Boar said as I gently shook Hercules and Cee to wake them. "Don't really need to work. Why should I? Acorns grow on trees."

When I told Hercules he'd just had a near-death experience, he laughed. "No way! I was just having a little nap."

I explained to the boar how he needed to go with Hercules to see King Eury.

"No offense, Boar," Cee said, "but Hercules is a big hero. He can't march into Mycenae with what looks like a big pink pig. It would ruin his image."

"How about if I roll in the dirt, scuff up my hooves, and point my tusks out?" The Boar made a terrible, frightening face.

"Works for me," said Cee.

"Awesome!" said Hercules.

When Hercules led the result of Labor IV through the gates of Mycenae, Boar let rip with one mighty roar after another. He was a real crowd pleaser.

"Eury!" called Hercules when they reached the palace. "Stick your head out of the pot and look upon the Wild Boar of Erymanthus!"

But as usual, Eury just peeked through the little slit.

"Okay," said the king. "I'll check off Boar. Now take him away. Far away from Erymanthus!" He pushed something out through the slit. "Here's your next labor, Hercules!"

Cee caught the thing before it fell to the ground. It was a small kamara Polarios (old Greek speak for "Polaroid camera") with a little roll of parchment attached to it. He unrolled the parchment and read: "Labor V: The neighbors of King Augeias have been complaining about a horrible stink. You have one day to muck out the king's stables. P.S. Bring me a picture showing them nice and clean."

(See? I told you Hercules wasn't finished mucking.)

"No problem!" said Hercules. "I spent years mucking out cow barns."

A laugh wafted up from inside the big bronze pot. Eury called, "You haven't seen these stables, Hercules!"

Hercules, Cee, and Hydra took off for Elis,

where King Augeias ruled. But the boar sat down beside the big bronze pot. I stuck around for a minute to see what would happen.

"I had a bronze pot once, King Eury," said Boar. "But the darned thing kept tarnishing. So I had to polish it. I don't really like polishing things. The polish smells bad, for one thing. You may not think so, but we boars have very sensitive snouts. The polish made my snout itch, and when my snout itches, it makes me sneeze."

"Guards!" called Eury from inside the pot. "Guards?"

CHAPTER XII
REALLY BIG JOB

I caught up with Hercules and the others. For a change, I walked with them to Elis. All I knew about King Augeias was that he owned a lot of cattle. And twelve prized white bulls sacred to Helios, the sun god. But as we went, we heard an earful about what to expect when we reached Augeias's stables.

"The stables are that way," said a group of hikers we'd stopped and asked for directions. "Hope you brought your nose plugs."

"Headed for the stables, eh?" said an old woman we met crossing a bridge over the River Alpheus. "I'd turn back if I were you."

"The stables?" said some ancient Greek picnickers we met as we waded across the Peneius

River at a shallow spot. They shook their heads. "No way!"

When we reached Elis, we didn't need to ask directions anymore. We just followed our noses halfway up a mountainside to King Augeias's estate. The whole place stank to high Mount Olympus.

The king lived in a big blue stone palace. His stables stretched from the very top of the mountain all the way down to the bottom.

Hercules strode up to the palace. "Hello, King Augeias!" he shouted.

For a while, no one answered him. Then the head of an ancient mortal appeared at an upper window. The crown on his head told us that we'd found the king.

"Are you rabble rousers?" the monarch called. "Come to make trouble for an old king?"

"No, sir!" said Hercules.

"Speak up!" said the old king.

"I have been sent to clean out your stables!" shouted Hercules.

"Ah!" said the king. "For XX years, I have

prayed to Hera to send a stable cleaner my way. At last! My prayers have been answered."

Hercules swallowed. XX *years*?

"Go on, then," said the old king. "Get to it."

"Sir?" said Hercules. "Tell me — how can you stand the stink?"

"Can't hear you!" shouted the old king. "I've lost my hearing now, along with my sense of smell. Speak up!"

Ah, that explained it.

"Never mind," said Hercules. "I'm on it."

We walked up the mountain to the first stable. Hercules opened the door. The stench was so powerful, it knocked us all off our feet.

"Ugh!" said Hercules. "These stables are worse than I thought."

"Much worse," said Cee, who looked as if he might pass out.

Hydra pinched two of her noses.

I had to agree with them. These stables were worse than anything I'd imagined.

The poor cattle! They were standing up to their necks in muck. But they must have been used to it, for they calmly chewed on their hay from racks attached to the stable walls at head level. Some of them might have been the white bulls of Helios. But in all that muck, who could tell?

"Anybody see a shovel?" asked Hercules. Our hero was ready to start mucking.

"Hercules, even *you* can't possibly shovel out all these stables in a single day," Cee pointed out.

"I have to," said Hercules. "Or I will have failed at my labors."

While they argued, I assessed the situation. It looked pretty grim.

Suddenly, Hydra started making wild gestures.

"What are you doing, Hydra?" asked Hercules.

Hydra kept gesturing.

"She's trying to tell us something," said Cee. "But what?"

No one could figure out what she meant.

Hercules brightened. "Are you playing charades?"

Hydra nodded eagerly. She held up two

fingers, pulled on an ear, and spread her arms wide.

"Two words," said Hercules. "First one sounds like 'big.' Pig? Jig? Rig?"

Hydra shook her heads. She pretended to — what? Shovel something?

"Dig!" said Hercules.

Hydra's heads nodded. She held up two fingers.

"Second word," said Hercules.

Hydra pointed north to the Alpheus River. Then to the Peneius River to the west.

Technically, pointing is not allowed in charades. But no one objected.

"River!" shouted Hercules. "Dig river!"

All Hydra's heads started nodding like crazy.

"Are you saying," said Cee, "that Hercules should dig new channels for the two rivers and get them to flow through the stables and wash them out?"

Hydra nodded so vigorously that several of her heads knocked together.

I smiled. Hydra wasn't much to look at, but

with all those heads, she sure had a lot of brain power. She'd just come up with a brilliant idea. There was only one problem with it: Hercules couldn't possibly dig fast enough to divert those rivers in a single day.

Luckily, I, too, had a brilliant idea.

"Be back in a flash," I told Hercules.

"Don't you want to dig a little first?" hinted Hercules.

"Later," I said. I knew Hercules thought I was trying to get out of helping him. But I also knew he'd thank me later. I walked swiftly to the Alpheus River and astro-traveled to its source.

ZIP!

There sat Alpheus, the river god, himself. He was young, as river gods go, and handsome. He had a full head of red hair and a bushy red beard.

"Alpheus?" I said. "Hades here."

Alpheus's watery blue eyes opened wide in surprise. "Hades!" he boomed. "Greetings. What an unexpected surprise. How's your brother Poseidon? That rascal hasn't been around to see me for years. Did you see my current today? It's full of the most enticing ripples."

River gods, as a rule, are very full of themselves, and Alpheus was no exception.

He leaned forward. "You know the goddess Artemis?"

"Well enough," I told him.

Alpheus sighed. "She splashed across me this morning, chasing a herd of antelope. It was a thrill, having her lovely feet running along my pebbles!"

I'd heard that Alpheus had a big crush on Artemis. Evidently it was true.

"I'm hoping she'll come this way again on her way back to her hunting lodge," said Alpheus. "Maybe she won't be in such a hurry. Maybe she'll do a little wading."

"She'll probably go home by way of King Augeias's place," I said. "It's quicker."

Alpheus raised his bushy red eyebrows. "Really? That's just beyond my banks."

"You could overflow your banks and get closer to the palace," I suggested. "That wouldn't be hard for a powerful river god like you. Then she'd have to cross you again."

Alpheus frowned. "Are you talking flood here?"

I shrugged. "It would be a bold move on your part," I told him. "But that's just the sort of move Artemis really goes for."

Alpheus started nodding. "You know, I think you're on to something." He stood up. "Excuse me, will you Hades?"

He raised his great, muscular arms and dove into his own waters.

I quickly chanted again.

ZIP!

I landed at the headwaters of the Peneius River. And there was Peneius, sitting on his moss-covered stone throne. He was staring moodily into the eddies of his water. His hair and beard had gone completely white since the last time I'd seen him. He gave a start when I appeared.

"Hades!" he said when he realized who it was. "Well, I'll be dammed. Ha-ha! Just a little river-god joke. Get it? So what brings you out this way?"

"Just checking on some earthly matters," I told him. "How are things with you, Peneuis?"

"Same old, same old," said Peneuis. "Can't complain, really. But if I could, I'd say I'm flowing a little low these days. A little low and a little slow. I'm not the river I once was, Hades."

"Hey, that's not what I heard," I told him. "Why, I'll bet you could still overflow your banks if you wanted to. Get a little choppy. Muster up a few whitecaps."

Peneius shook his white-maned head. "I don't know."

"Alpheus is only a little younger than you are," I pointed out. "And he's flooding today."

"Alpheus?" Peneius sat straight up in his throne. "You know that for a fact?"

"Saw him dive into his river with my own eyes," I said. "He was going to try to send a stream rushing down through King Augeias's property."

"No kidding." Peneius was wide awake now.

"You could flood there, too," I said. "And if, at the end of the day, some of his waters happened to end up in your river and raised your water level . . . well, it wouldn't be your fault."

"I'd have high waters again," said Peneius, half to himself. "Good to talk to you, Hades. Very helpful." He stood up, swinging his arms in preparation for a swan dive. "Send my best to that brother of yours, won't you? Now, if you'll excuse me?"

"Go ahead," I said. "Have a great flood!"

ZIP!

I went straight back to Hercules. He was digging on the banks of the Alpheus River for all he was worth. Cee was digging beside him. Hydra was mapping out how the canal should flow.

"Flood warning," I told him. "The rivers are about to flow through the stables."

"Hercules!" said Cee. "Go tell the cattle to grab their feed troughs with their teeth, and hold on tight. Hurry!"

"Moooo! Maaaa maaaah mooo!" Hercules cried as he ran off to spread the word.

Soon a rushing, roaring sound filled the air. Then, from the crest of the hill, came two giant waves. Hercules was a powerful swimmer. I knew he'd be okay. But Cee was a lion — a big cat — and had a cat's fear of water. Hydra would survive any flood, but I worried that she might get battered. So, though it was against the rules of *How Immortals Can and Can't Help Mortals*, I put my arms around those two and chanted again.

ZIP!

We landed on the roof of King Augeias's palace. And from there, we had the perfect view of the raging rivers whooshing down the hill. Their clear waters rushed into the stables. Minutes later, thick, gooey glop flowed out of the stables at the bottom of the hill. In an hour the whole thing was over.

Hydra remembered to snap a picture: *CLICK! Buzzzzzz.* It was a perfect shot.

This time, as Hercules walked through the gates of Mycenae, he had no monster to show off to the crowds. Still, the mortals cheered him.

He didn't need a monster anymore. Hercules had grown stronger and more muscular with every labor. Now, he was the main attraction.

"You're our hero, Hercules!" shouted the bystanders.

"Eury!" called Hercules, rapping on the big bronze pot. "Come and see the picture of the nice, clean stables!"

"Slide it to me," said Eury. He opened the slot. Hercules stuck in the picture.

"Can't believe it," Eury muttered. "But I'll check it off."

I was wearing my helmet. I didn't want Eury to know I was giving Hercules a hand. But fall was almost over. I'd promised Persephone I'd be home by the first day of winter. Time was running out. I had to speed things up, so I took a chance and called invisibly, "Give him his next labor!"

"Here you go," said Eury. He laughed again as he pushed a little roll of parchment through the slot. "Good luck with the birdies!"

CHAPTER XIII
BIG BIRD

"Labor VI," read Cee as we headed out of the city gates again. "Get rid of the Stymphalian birds who are befouling everything around them." He frowned. "Stymphalian birds? Never heard of them."

"Me neither," said Hercules.

Hydra shook her head.

"I guess that makes me the bearer of bad news," I told them. "The Stymphalian birds live in a marsh in Arcadia. They're huge and have iron beaks and iron wings. There are so many of them that when they fly in circles over the marsh, they blot out the sun, and the earth turns dark as night. But that's not the worst thing about them."

"I'm afraid to ask," said Cee.

"They can fire their iron wing feathers like arrows," I said. "They shoot mortals, pick them up in their iron claws, and rip them apart with their iron beaks. But that's not the worst thing about them."

"Don't tell us!" said Cee.

"The worst thing about them," I said, "is their deadly poisonous Stymphalian birdie doo."

"More muck?" said Hercules.

Hydra signed what I took to be something close to "Yuck."

Cee wrinkled his nose.

But Hercules, Cee, and Hydra marched bravely off to the Arcadian marsh. As usual, I met them there.

ZIP!

Brrrrr! It was freezing. I found Hercules running around the swamp, trying to catch the birds with his hands. He wasn't having any luck. Cee and Hydra stood shivering miserably at the edge of the frigid marsh. Cee had a paw clapped over his nose. Hydra had managed to fashion nose clips out of twigs. She wore one on each of her nine noses.

The Stymphalian birds were shivering, too. The birds that didn't have their heads tucked under their iron wings had icicles hanging off their beaks.

Hydra waded over to me. She held up two fingers.

"Two words," I said, watching her closely. "First word is . . ."

Hydra made fluttering, flapping motions with her arms.

"Fly," I said.

Hydra gave me a thumbs-up. I'd gotten it, first try! Again, she held up two fingers.

"Second word," I said.

Hydra pulled on an earlobe, then pointed to her mouth.

"Sounds like . . . mouth?"

Hydra nodded.

"Fly mouth." That was nonsense. But Hydra was nodding. I had to be close. "Fly south."

Thumbs-up from Hydra.

"Fly south!" I said, getting as excited as Hydra. "Yes! If we can get them to fly south, we'll be rid of them."

"At least until next spring," Cee pointed out.

"Whatever," said Hercules, who had waded out of the marsh when he saw what Hydra was up to. "But how do we get them to fly south?"

If ever a situation called for CCC this was it. "Give me a minute," I said as I switched my brain into Creature Communication Channel. *Leader of the Stymphalian birds, come here please. It's me, Hades, King of the Underworld. I want to talk to you.*

I heard some pretty awful screeching and static inside my brain. Then one of the birds began wading toward me. It was an enormous creature. Its iron wings pressed up against its body of gray metal feathers. It had a short neck and, for a bird, a large head with a dull iron beak.

F-F-F-Ferrica here, she said through her chattering beak.

Cold, eh? I said.

F-f-f-freezing. Ferrica puffed up her gray feathers to warm herself.

Why don't you and the flock fly south for the winter? I asked her.

Leave the m-m-m-marsh? she asked.

Sure, I replied. *Fly south, where it's nice and warm. That's what most birds do when the weather turns cold.*

No one ever t-t-t-told me, said Ferrica. *Which way is s-s-south?*

I pointed. *You won't regret it.*

Th-th-thanks, Ferrica said.

Just don't go too far south, I thought after her as she turned and waded back into the marsh. *Iron can get pretty hot.*

Ferrica began squawking. Soon the whole stinky flock began flapping in preparation for takeoff.

"Go, you Stinkphalian birdies!" yelled Hercules. He ran around the marsh yelling and whooping and making as much racket as possible to get those birds to fly.

Then, as if on a signal, each and every

Stymphalian bird flapped its iron wings and rose up into the air. As the birds circled overhead, the sky turned dark as midnight.

"Careful!" Cee shouted over the whir of iron wings. "Don't let them you-know-what on you!"

The birds flew off toward the south, and the sun reappeared.

CLICK! Buzzzz. Hydra snapped a picture of the birdless swamp.

"They're gone!" cried Hercules. "Thanks, Hades!"

"Don't mention it," I said. "Listen, Hercules, it's time for me to go down to the Underworld for the winter."

"All right," said Hercules. "Have a good one, Uncle Hades."

"I won't be around to help with your labors," I pointed out.

"That's okay," said Hercules.

"You could wait until spring to go back to Eury," I said. "Then I'll be back to, you know, do what I can for you."

"Nah, you go, Uncle Hades," said Hercules.

"Well, here's a phone," I said. Demeter, who long ago, had invented the little phones so she could keep track of Persephone, had made all of us gods promise never to give a phone to a mortal. I couldn't let Hercules have it, so I handed it to Hydra. "If there's any problem — anything at all — call me, day or night. My number is on memory dial I."

"We'll be fine on our own, Uncle Hades," said Hercules. "Bye!"

I have to say I felt sort of left out as I watched the three turn and start back to Mycenae.

CHAPTER XIV

BIG GIRDLE

"Welcome home, Lord Hades!" said Charon, the old ferryman, as he poled me back across the River Styx to my kingdom.

"Thank you, Charon." I sighed as I put a gold coin into his hand and drove my steeds off the ferry. Not that I wasn't glad to be home. I was! And I couldn't wait to greet Persephone when she came home the following day. But it was hard — very hard — leaving Hercules and his crew up on earth to go on their next adventure without me.

There was only one thing that could have cheered me up right then, and here he came, bounding toward my chariot — my own underdog, Cerberus. He ran and leaped into my lap, giving me the old triple face-lick.

"Ah, Cerbie," I said. "I've missed you, too. You're my fine dog, dog, dog."

It turned out to be a wonderful winter. Persephone and I hung out in the great room, reading in front of the fire. We took long walks in Elysium among the apple trees. We had several excellent dinners at the Underworld Grill. Yet every time my phone rang, I half hoped it would be Hydra, saying that Hercules needed me. But all winter long, she never called.

When spring rolled around, I drove Persephone back up to earth.

"So long, Hades," Persephone said when I dropped her off at the little apartment she kept in Athens. "It was a cozy winter, don't you think?"

"Perfect," I told her. When she was settled in, I drove to Mycenae to look for Hercules. I found him, Cee, and Hydra as they were leaving the city.

Cee told me that Hercules had finished two labors all on his own. I couldn't believe it. For Labor VII, he and his buddies went to Crete, where a bull belonging to King Minos had gone mad and was running wild, stampeding everything in sight. Hercules chased down the bull and had a good, long talk with him in Cow. Then, just for show, he slung him over his shoulders and paraded through the streets of Knossos all the way to King Minos's palace. The crowds cheered him like crazy. At least that's the way Hercules told it.

I wasn't all that sorry that I'd missed Labor VIII. Hercules had to get rid of the Mares of King Diomedes. All they knew about this king was that he was very fond of music. And that he fed his mares on the flesh of mortals, which turned them into savage beasts. (Is it power that makes so many mythological kings total whackos? Or are they born that way? I've never been able to decide.)

In any case, Hercules showed up on Diomedes's doorstep. When the king came to the door, Hercules began singing. *"Do re me fo foo fee foooo!"*

The music-loving Diomedes clapped his hand over his ears and ran away from the awful screeching. Hercules chased him to the seashore, singing all the way. The king plunged into the sea and was last seen doing the backstroke off the coast of what later became Spain.

Meanwhile, Cee gathered the mares together, fed them some oats, barley, carrots, flaxseed — a totally healthful vegetarian diet. In only a few days they calmed down and were content to graze and nibble grass.

"We just picked up Labor IX," Hercules told me. "I don't have to bring Eury any weird monster this time. All I have to do is get this queen's girdle. Piece of cake. Come on!"

"Whose girdle?" I asked, falling into step with them.

"Hippo —" He turned to Cee. "Hippo who?"

"Hippolyta," Cee said. "Queen of the Amazons."

I frowned. "I don't like it."

"What's wrong?" said Hercules. "I can just ask her for her girdle. It'll be easy!"

"Too easy," I grumbled. "There must be a catch."

I went with them as far as the harbor. It was the off season, so they got an amazingly good deal on renting a big cruise ship, the *Warrior Princess*, complete with crew. They got ready to sail it to the land of the Amazons. I avoid boat travel whenever possible, so I put on my Helmet of Darkness. *POOF!* And — *ZIP!* — astro-traveled to Amazon Harbor.

I arrived early so I could check out the place. I'd heard about the land of the Amazons, where women ruled and men did all the household chores, but I'd never been there myself. I walked along a riverbank. It was lined with men. Some of them had waded into the water and were washing clothes. Others were beating clothes with rocks — an early form of stain removal. Still other men were laying clothes out on rocks to dry. I walked on to the village. There, men had built fires and set cooking pots over them. They stood stirring the pots, jiggling toddlers on their hips, exchanging recipes, and talking about how they hoped the women would return from their hunt with plenty of game.

After a few days, I heard the men talking excitedly over their cooking pots about a large cruise ship that had been seen heading for the harbor. I went to meet it — invisibly of course. As Hercules and company rowed from the ship, an army of female warriors gathered on the shore. This was the first I'd seen of them. They were all tall and blond. They wore the skins of wild beasts and carried big brass bows and half-moon-shaped shields. Each had a quiver of arrows slung over her shoulder.

Leading the troops stood an Amazon who was a head taller than any of the others. She had on a sleeveless fur tunic that hit her just above the knees. Around her waist she wore a wide golden girdle. No wonder Eury had asked Hercules to get it for him. It was a stunner, set with diamonds, emeralds, and pearls. I wondered if she'd give it up so easily.

"Greetings, strangers!" the tall Amazon called as Hercules, Cee, and Hydra climbed out of the rowboat and waded ashore. "I am Hippolyta, Queen of the Amazons."

Hercules stared at her and smiled a goofy smile. Hippolyta was as tall as he was. Her sleeveless outfit showed off some nice-sized biceps. It wasn't hard to tell what Hercules was thinking: here was a girl he could arm wrestle!

"Why have you come to our shore?" asked Hippolyta.

Hercules continued to smile his goofy smile.

Cee stepped forward. "Greetings, Queen!" he said. "We come in peace!"

"Awwww!" came a chorus of disappointed groans from Hippolyta's troops. Clearly they'd been hoping to fight a big battle against these strangers.

Hippolyta turned to her warriors. "Troops, dis-MISS!"

The warriors turned and marched off toward the village.

Hippolyta turned back to Hercules. "How about giving me a tour of your boat?"

"No problem!" said Hercules.

The two of them raced to the rowboat.

"We're coming, too!" shouted Cee. Hydra

jumped on his back, and they took off after Hercules.

After a little disagreement about who would row, Hippolyta sat down, picked up the oars, and rowed quickly to the *Warrior Princess*. No one suspected that there was an invisible fifth passenger aboard — me.

When we reached the ship, everyone climbed up a rope ladder. I followed right behind.

Hercules gave a quick tour of the ship. "These are the masts," he said, pointing.

"Tall," said Queen Hippolyta.

"And these are the decks," said Hercules.

"Flat," said Queen Hippolyta. "Rowing made me hungry. What's to eat?"

A crew member served them lunch. Hercules and Hippolyta sat down and dug in. I hovered invisibly nearby, helping myself when I saw the chance. After some small talk about how many push-ups he could do, and how many chin-ups she could do, Hercules got down to business.

"I picked the hard path in life," he began.

"Can I have more chips?" said Hippolyta.

"So I have to do XII practically impossible labors," said Hercules.

"Pass the pickles," said Hippolyta.

"I've run off monsters and cleaned out really yucky stables," said Hercules.

"If you don't want those last cheese curls, I'll take them," said Hippolyta, reaching.

"For Labor IX I'm supposed to get your girdle," said Hercules.

"Waa huuuurgle?" Hippolyta swallowed her cheese curls. "My girdle? But why?"

Hercules shrugged. "That's just what it said on the slip of parchment. I'm supposed to get your girdle and take it to the king of Mycenae."

"I don't know," Hippolyta frowned. "This girdle was a present from Ares. You know, god of war? Would you bring it back?"

"I could try," said Hercules.

"Okay," said Hippolyta. She unfastened her golden girdle and handed it to Hercules.

Hercules smiled. "I told Hades this was going to be easy."

Hippolyta shrugged as she grabbed another

handful of chips. "If I don't get it back, my warriors and I will sail to Mycenae, set fire to the city, kidnap the king, and bring him back here to scrub the palace floors."

"Sounds fair to me," said Hercules.

Then they settled down to do some serious eating.

Hippolyta looked up first. "What's that noise?" she asked.

Hercules listened. "It sounds like an army rowing this way with clinking spears and clanking battle-axes."

They jumped up and ran to the side of the boat. I was right on their heels. The harbor was filled with Amazon rowboats! Each boat was filled with Amazon warriors. They were brandishing spears and battle-axes and shouting: "Surrender, Hercules!"

CHAPTER XV
BIG GOODBYE

"We're out of here!" yelled Hercules.

He ran to the ropes and began hoisting the sails.

Queen Hippolyta stayed at the railing. "What's wrong?" she shouted to her warriors. "What's going on?"

What indeed? I joined Hippolyta at the rails. The Amazon boats were closing in. Soon they'd be bumping our hull. Some of the warriors had drawn back their bowstrings. They were ready to fire.

"Onward, mighty warriors!" cried the lead Amazon, pumping her fist in the air and shouting viciously. She wore a horned helmet, but her hair blew out from under it, so I couldn't see her face. "How dare they steal our queen!" she shouted. "How dare they kidnap Hippolyta?"

Steal? Kidnap? What was this warrior ranting about? Wait a minute! Who was that warrior, anyway? I looked harder. That hair — it was Hera!

I ran to the ship's wheel. Hercules had grabbed the wheel from a frantic crew member and was attempting to steer the *Warrior Princess* away from the Amazon war boats. I whipped off my helmet.

"Uncle Hades!" exclaimed Hercules. "The Amazons are after us!"

"Three guesses who's leading the chase," I said. "And the first two don't count."

Hercules wrinkled his brow in thought. "Okay, um . . . so how many guesses is that?"

"Never mind!" I shouted. "It's Hera. She must have spread a rumor among the Amazons that you've kidnapped their queen."

"Dang," said Hercules, quickly turning the wheel to the right to dodge a rowboat filled with angry Amazons. "I guess getting that girdle isn't so easy after all."

Our ship wasn't moving fast enough. The Amazons were catching up.

I pulled out my cell phone. I hit memory dial for my brother, Poseidon. I listened as the phone rang and rang. I hoped I wouldn't get his machine.

"Ruler of the Seas," Poseidon answered at last.

"Po!" I shouted into the phone. "It's Hades. Thank Mount Olympus I reached you. I need your help."

"Where are you, bro?" asked Po.

"I'm on board the *Warrior Princess*."

"Excellent vessel," said Po.

"We're pulling out of Amazon Harbor. We've got Queen Hippolyta aboard."

"I hear she's a real babe!"

"The wind's against us!" I shouted into the phone.

"Is she a babe, Hades? Is she?"

"Yes!" I shouted. "Listen, Po, there are about a hundred boatloads of angry Amazons chasing us!"

"Are they all babes?"

"PO! We need help!"

"Do what I can, big bro. Sounds like I should send some waves to swamp them and get a couple of wind gods to speed you away."

"That would be great, Po. Thanks!"

I looked out at the Amazon boats. Hera was in the lead. She was shaking her fist and yelling. I was glad I was too far away to hear what she was saying.

Now Hippolyta ran to the wheel. "There's an imposter in the first boat!" she cried. "You must turn back! We must vanquish her!"

"Not a good idea," I said.

Hippolyta turned and noticed me for the first time. "Who are you? And who asked you?"

"I'm Hades," I told her. "And the imposter is Hera. You're strong, and you've got big muscles, Hippolyta. But you're no match for a goddess."

"I hear you," said Hippolyta. "But why is Hera doing this? I always sacrifice to her."

"She's after me," said Hercules.

"How did you offend Hera?" asked Hippolyta.

"By being born," said Hercules.

"Mmm . . ." said the queen. "Not much you can do about that."

A sudden gust of wind filled our sails. We began speeding over the waves.

"All right," shouted Hercules as we raced across the water and away from the Amazon navy.

At the same time, the sea began roiling with huge waves. They broke over the Amazon war boats, soaking the warriors. At last the Amazons turned their boats and began rowing for the shore.

I owed my bro Po big time.

"I must go back and speak to my warriors," said Hippolyta. "Tell them about Hera. Hey, what's that?"

She pointed to something in the distance.

I squinted and made out Poseidon's cherry-red sea chariot, pulled by his team of giant sea horses. In no time, he drew up alongside our ship.

"I see the winds I sent did the trick." Po grinned at Hippolyta.

"They did," said Hercules. "Thanks!"

Hippolyta grinned back at Po. "I'll bet that chariot can really fly!"

"Hop in," said Po. "I'll take you for a spin."

"You're on." Hippolyta climbed up onto the railing of the *Warrior Princess* and leaped into Po's chariot. She turned back and waved. "Goodbye, Hercules!" she called. "Goodbye!"

CHAPTER XVI

BIG BURN

"See you!" Hercules waved as Hippolyta sped off with Po. He watched until they were no more than a red speck on the horizon. "Dang!" he said. "I thought she liked me."

"She did, Hercules," I said, patting him on the shoulder. "I could tell. But it's hard to compete with a god. Especially one with a bright-red sea chariot."

"At least you got the girdle," said Cee, coming up to take a turn at the wheel.

Hydra made a few hand signals that seemed to mean, *She ate too much anyway.*

By the time we reached Mycenae, Hercules had pretty much gotten over Hippolyta. He marched proudly through the city gates holding the jeweled girdle high over his head, showing it to the crowd. All the onlookers ooohed and aaahed.

"Eury!" Hercules called when he reached the palace. "Come out of the pot! A girdle can't hurt you."

"Just put it down, Hercules," Eury called from inside the pot. "I'll have my people pick it up." Then he slid a piece of parchment out through the slot. "Here's Labor X. Get to work, Hercules!"

Cee unrolled the parchment. "Holy cow!" he said. "More cows."

"I like cows," said Hercules.

"Then you'll like this one," said Cee. And he read: "Labor X: Fetch the red cattle of Geryon, and bring them to me."

"No problem!" said Hercules, and the trio turned back toward the city gates. "Where's Geryon?"

Geryon wasn't a where. Geryon was a who. I'd had to tell Hercules about the Stymphalian birds. But I decided not to break the bad news about Geryon. There were just some things that

Hercules was going to have to find out on his own.

I headed back to my kingdom for a while. When I got a message from Po that Hercules and company had rented a small ship and sailed almost all the way to the west coast of Iberia — *ZIP!* — I came invisibly aboard.

Whew! It was like an oven on that ship. The sun was beating down. There wasn't a cloud in the sky.

Hercules stood at the wheel, red-faced and covered with sweat. He was grumbling loudly about the sun and how Helios ought to drive his flaming chariot higher in the sky so it wouldn't be so hot down below. I hardly blamed Hercules. Three burning hot days at sea in a small boat, and I would have been grumbling, too. Cee was stretched out in the stern, fanning himself. Hydra had squished herself under a seat, the only place she could find any shade.

Suddenly Hercules let go of the wheel. He grabbed his bow, put in an arrow, and aimed it at the sun. "Look out, Helios!" he shouted.

"Hercules! Don't shoot!" I lunged for him. But I didn't make it in time.

He fired at the chariot of the sun.

I watched in helpless horror as the arrow rose swiftly into the sky. It struck the flank of one of Helios's steeds. The arrow didn't stick, but the horse reared and whinnied in surprise. The other seven horses began to buck and whinny, too. They snorted flames that shot across the sky, turning it orange. A roar like thunder rumbled.

"Ooops!" Hercules turned his face up to the sky. "Sorry, Helios! Forgive me!"

At least he had the sense to apologize. But it was too little, too late. Once again, it was U.H.T.T.R.

I chanted the astro-traveling spell. *ZIP!* I found myself clinging to the rear bumper of Helios's chariot. He was going about CC dekamiles an hour. I hung on tight. Talk about hot. How did Helios stand the heat, day after day? I inched forward, hand over hand, and knocked on the passenger-side window. Helios leaned over and opened the door.

"Hey, it's air-conditioned!" I exclaimed as I slid inside.

"Shut the door," said Helios, never taking his orange eyes off the Sky Highway. "It can heat up pretty fast." He'd calmed his steeds by this time. "So who's the genius down there taking potshots at my horses?"

"Hercules," I said. "He's got a little temper problem." I explained about Hera, King Eurystheus, and the XII Labors. "He's my nephew — Zeus's son. Think you could let this one go?"

Helios shook his mane of wild orange hair. "I don't think so, Hades. No one shoots the sun and gets away with it."

"Helios," I said, "did I mention that it was Hercules who cleaned out the stables where you keep your twelve white bulls?"

"No kidding?" said Helios. "Well, that changes everything. My bulls have never been so frisky. But, Hades, if Hercules tries anything like this again, I'll give him a sunburn he'll never forget."

CHAPTER XVII
BIG MATCH

I rode with Helios for a while. The view from his sky chariot was amazing. Then — *ZIP!* — I astro-traveled back to Hercules. He and his crew were making their way up Mount Abas to Geryon's castle.

"Sorry, Uncle Hades," muttered Hercules. "Is Helios's horse okay?"

"He's fine," I said. "And Helios has agreed to forgive you — this time."

"There won't be a next time!" Hercules said. "I promise."

"Heads up!" shouted Cee. "Looks like Geryon's got a dog!"

An enormous, two-headed dog came rushing at us.

"Sic 'em, Orthus!" Geryon shouted angrily from the top of the mountain. "Chew 'em to bits!"

The monstrous dog was bearing down on us. Both his mouths were open wide. He was snarling, showing row after row of pointed, shark-like teeth. He lashed his mighty tail, tipped with a barbed wrecking ball.

Hercules bent his knees slightly, getting in position to grab the dog when it leapt at him.

Suddenly all of Hydra's necks shot out to the full length. She jumped into the dog's path.

"Kill, Orthus!" commanded Geryon. "Kill!"

Hydra stretched her arms wide, and the great, snarling beast jumped into them. Orthus began licking head after little head, drooling with happiness to be reunited with Hydra, his monstrous sister.

"Orthus!" yelled Geryon. "Bite! Scratch! Destroy!"

But Orthus just kept licking.

I glanced over at Geryon. He was exactly as I remembered him. He called himself the Strongest Man on Earth. Strong, yes. But man? That was a bit of a stretch. Starting from the ground up, Geryon looked like a man. He had two feet. Two legs. Hips, a waist. But then things got a little wonky. Three torsos sprouted from his waist. Each one had a set of arms and its own head. Geryon was also known as I, II, III. He was a triple threat.

"Hey, Hercules!" called I. "I'll wrestle you for my herd."

"You're on, Geryon!" Hercules started running up the mountain.

Now someone stepped up next to Geryon. "Meet my coach," said II.

Three guesses who his coach was. First two don't count.

"Not that I need a coach," added III.

"Uncle Hades?" said Hercules, his eyes fastened on Hera. "Want to be my coach?"

"Absolutely." I smiled. Hera was a powerful goddess with a grudge. But she knew next to nothing about wrestling. Whereas, I, Hades, knew just about everything.

I put Cee to work massaging Hercules's

shoulders. I told Hydra to keep her eighteen eyes on Geryon, looking for weaknesses.

"You can take him," I told Hercules.

"No problem," said Hercules. But he didn't sound so sure.

"Go for I or III," I advised. "But try to keep away from II. If II gets you down, I and III will pile on."

"Got it," said Hercules.

Suddenly Hydra ran over. She held up two fingers.

"Two words?" said Hercules.

Hydra gave him a thumbs-up. Then she held up one finger and spread her arms wide.

"First word . . . huge?" said Hercules.

Hydra shook her heads.

"Big?" Hercules guessed.

Thumbs-up from Hydra. Now she held up two fingers, pulled her ear, and shook her head.

"Second word. Sounds like . . . " Hercules scrunched up his face. "No?"

Thumbs-up again!

"Big no. Big Joe?" guessed Hercules. "Big moe? Big foe?"

Hydra shook her head.

"Big woe? Big bow? Big . . . toe?"

Thumbs-up!

Hercules glanced over at Geryon. He saw a bulge on the front of Geryon's left shoe.

"On it," he said.

The wrestlers began circling one another. The way Geryon was built, it looked like a tag-team match. Suddenly, II grabbed Hercules and flipped him onto his back. Hercules wriggled out of the hold and jumped up. He charged across the ring, bounced off the ropes, and catapulted back to Geryon, stomping on his left big toe.

"AAAAAAAAAAAAAAAAAAAAAAAAAAA AAAAYYYYYYYYYYYYYYYYYYYYYYYYYYYYYY!" screamed I, II and III. All three torsos hit the mat. Hercules didn't waste a second. He jumped on them and held them down for the count.

"The winner is — Hercules!" I held up his hand in victory.

Geryon stayed down on the mat, moaning and holding his toe. "Oh, man," he groaned. "I think you popped my blister!"

"For Mount Olympus's sake, Geryon," said

Hera, clearly disgusted with her protégé. "Get over it!"

After that, Hercules spoke to Geryon's cows, and they agreed to come along to Mycenae. Cee had some problems finding a ship big enough to hold the whole herd, but at last he was successful, and off they sailed. I wanted to keep an eye on Hercules, so I went, too. The only excitement came on the first night of the trip, when we all heard a wild scratching noise coming from under the bow.

"Rats down below, I'll wager," said the ship's captain.

But when he opened the hold, out bounded Orthus.

The enormous two-headed dog and his nine-headed blob of a sister spent the rest of the voyage together.

When Hercules marched through the gates of Mycenae, leading a procession of some MCC red cows, it was quite a scene. The mortals of Mycenae cheered Hercules so loudly that they were all hoarse for a week.

"Eury!" called Hercules when he reached the palace. "Labor X is done!"

The slot slid open. "Holy cow!" Eury exclaimed. "I'll check it off the list."

CHAPTER XVIII

BIG CHAIR

"Labor XI," read Cee, after Eury had handed him yet another piece of parchment. "Bring me the golden apples from the garden of the Hesperides."

"Let's go apple picking!" said Hercules.

With the addition of Orthus, there were four in the party now. It was a formidable-looking crew: a larger-than-life muscle-bound hero, a lion, a nine-headed monster, and a two-headed, shark-toothed, barbed-wrecking-ball-tailed dog. Off they went to find the garden of the Hesperides.

"Hercules," I said as I walked invisibly out of the city with them. "It's winter again. I must return home to my Underworld kingdom. Just a few words before I go."

"Okay, Uncle Hades," said Hercules. "Whatever."

"Not 'whatever,' Hercules," I said. "Pay attention! This is important. Very important. The garden of the Hesperides is a long way from here, on the slope of Mount Atlas. The Titan Atlas is the only one around who knows the exact location of the garden. You'll have to go to him, and ask him to tell you. Now, here's the tricky part. The tree that bears the golden apples belongs to Hera."

"Figures," said Hercules.

"Our Granny Gaia, Mother Earth, gave the tree to Hera as a wedding present when she married Zeus," I went on. "Hera loves this tree so dearly that she's set a huge hundred-headed dragon to guard her precious apples."

"No problem," said Hercules.

"Hercules!" I said. "This won't be easy." I turned to Cee and Hydra. "Whatever he does, he must not pick the apples himself. Got it?"

"Got it," said Cee.

"You have my phone number," I said.

"Got it," said Cee again. "Don't worry about us. Have a good winter, Hades!"

I headed back down to the Underworld. To tell you the truth, I'd had enough of Hercules and his labors by now. All I wanted was to spend the winter sitting beside Persephone in front of a roaring fire with Cerbie at our feet.

I was a week late getting home. Persephone was already there. And she was all upset.

"Thank Mount Olympus you're here!" she exclaimed.

"What's wrong, P-phone?" I'd never seen her so rattled.

"Two mortal heroes are here in the Underworld, Hades."

"Mortals? Impossible! They're not allowed in my kingdom. Cerberus would never let them in. Would you, Cerbie?" I eyed my guard dog of the Underworld. But he was suddenly very busy licking his flank.

Persephone folded her arms across her chest.

"They're here, Hades. And what's more, they sing under my window every night. Then one of them recites love poems!"

My mouth dropped open. I was shocked. I couldn't speak! Persephone wasn't much of a kidder. But surely she was joking.

"It's true, Hades," said Persephone, a twinkle in her eye now. "I have suitors. Wait until tonight. You'll hear from them yourself."

That night, Persephone climbed into bed. I sat in a chair beside the bed, waiting. Sure enough, I heard a rustling in the bushes below the bedroom window. Then two male voices began to sing:

"My love for you is like goat cheese,
darling mine!
It grows better with age and goes well
with red wine!"

That was all I needed to hear.

I stuck my head out the window. "Suitors!" I called. "What fine singing. Persephone is overjoyed to hear it."

"Hades!" Persephone whispered. "I am *not*!"

"Uh . . . Hades?" said one of the suitors.

"Oh, no!" said the other. "You said he was up on earth!"

I peered into the night. "*Theseus?*" I exclaimed. "Is that you?"

"Mmm . . ." said Theseus. "Yeah."

"Come!" I told him. "You and your friend, meet me around the back of the palace, on the porch. We need to talk."

I met them and ushered them onto the porch. I seldom sit there. But it was just right for this occasion. The porch ceiling is made of braided asphodel vines. Leaves hang down from it. Everything is moist and very mossy. I sat down on my old wooden throne. I motioned for Theseus and his friend to sit opposite me in a big double-size chair.

"Sorry, Hades," muttered Theseus.

"Oh, you were just having fun," I said. "Who's your friend?"

The other mortal spoke up. "I'm Peirithous," he said. "You are the dreaded Ruler of the Dead. I know you could kill me in an instant. But danger does not frighten me. I am in love with Lady Persephone."

"That makes two of us," I said. It was hard not to laugh. Who did this little pipsqueak mortal think he was, anyway?

"Theseus," I said shaking my head. "After all I did to help you."

"Did you?" said Theseus. "I can't remember." Theseus always was the world's most forgetful hero. When I was traveling with him, he'd forget his sandals if they weren't strapped onto his feet. But he was about to bring new meaning to the words *I forget*.

"I'll bet Hermes told you about the shortcut down to my kingdom."

"Uh . . . that sounds right, Hades," said Theseus. "But I'm not sure."

"And did you think you could help your friend lure Persephone away from me?"

Theseus thought hard. At last he said, "I forget."

I turned to Peirithous. "What about you?" I said. "Did you think your love songs would win Persephone's heart?"

"I — I can't say," said Peirithous. He looked terribly confused.

I stood up from my throne. "Sit there, and think about it for a while."

"No!" said Theseus. "I have deeds to do!"

"What deeds?" I asked.

He wrinkled his brow. "I, uh, I can't remember exactly what they are right now."

"But there are deeds!" said Peirithous. "We must be at them!"

I watched them struggle to rise from their stone chair. But they were stuck fast.

"You are sitting in the Chair of Forgetfulness," I told them. "You can never rise without my permission. The longer you sit there, the less you will remember. In fact, ten minutes from now, you won't remember that I told you this."
I turned to go.

"Come back!" called Theseus. "Whoever you are."

But I left them there with their muddled thoughts.

Persephone was sitting up in bed when I got back to our room.

"Your suitors are out on the porch," I told her. I sat down on the side of the bed and unbuckled my godly sandals. "I don't think they'll bother you with their love songs again."

Persephone smiled. "Thank you, Hades. You're all the suitor I need. Oh, I almost forgot. You had a phone call. From Hydra."

I'd told her to call, day or night. She'd picked night. "What did she say?"

"She needs you to come to the base of Mount Atlas, on the double."

I buckled up my sandals again. "I'll take care of this fast, Persephone. Then I'll come back here for the whole winter. No interruptions. I promise."

"Oh, sure, Hades," Persephone said. As I hurried away, she called, "Good luck!"

Mount Atlas was on earth. But I knew a way to get to its base through a remote part of my kingdom. I hitched up my steeds and quickly drove to it. By the time I got there, rosy dawn had dawned. I could see the Titan Atlas. He was bent way over under the weight of the sky, which he held on his broad shoulders. Holding up the sky was Atlas's punishment for being the captain of the Titan's kickstone team in the long-ago match against the gods. The game had gotten rough enough to wreck the earth and crack one of the four pillars that held up the sky. That's why Atlas had to hold it.

I hadn't seen Atlas in a long time. As I approached him now, he looked smaller than I remembered. I guessed all that weight pressing down on him had taken its toll. But as I drew closer, I saw that I'd been wrong. It wasn't Atlas holding the sky on his shoulders. It was Hercules!

CHAPTER XIX
BIG APPLE

Hercules's face had turned beet red from the effort of holding up the sky.

"Here comes Hades," Cee told Hercules as I approached. He and Hydra were standing helplessly beside our hero. "He'll know what to do."

I reined in my steeds. "Let me guess," I said. "You found Atlas. You felt like showing off and said you'd hold the sky for him if he'd go pick the golden apples for you."

"Something like that," Hercules grunted.

"And Atlas hasn't come back," I added.

"Right," said Hercules.

"But he will," said Cee. "He gave his word."

Hydra began pointing excitedly to the south.

I turned to look, and there came Atlas. He was whistling happily as he walked, juggling the three golden apples.

"Let me do the talking," I told the others as Atlas drew nearer.

"Hello!" Atlas sang out. Anyone could see how happy he was to be free and walking around again.

"Greetings, Atlas!" I called. "So, you picked the golden apples. I thought the apple tree was guarded by a fierce many-headed dragon. How did you manage it?"

"I waited until the dragon fell asleep," said Atlas. He looked over his shoulder, as if something might be coming after him. Then he turned to Hercules. "Listen, why don't I take these golden apples to the king for you. Tell me again — which king is it?"

"King Eurystheus," I said quickly. "That's so nice of you, Atlas. Could you do me a favor, though, before you go?"

"Happy to," said Atlas.

I jogged back to my chariot and picked up the

lap blanket I always carry in case there's a chill. I ran back with it to the others.

"Hercules isn't as mighty as you, Atlas," I said.

"No mortal is," he agreed.

"He isn't used to holding so much weight," I added as I folded the lap blanket in two. "I'd like to put this on his shoulders. You know, give him a little padding."

Atlas nodded. "Good idea."

"You're the only one strong enough to hold the sky for a minute while I slip this onto his shoulders," I said. "Would you mind?"

"Not a bit," Atlas put down the apples. Then he stood to the right of Hercules and bent down. Hercules leaned to the right, and the sky rolled off his shoulders and onto Atlas's again.

"Whoa!" exclaimed Hercules as he slowly straightened up again. "That was *heavy*."

"You'll get used to it," said Atlas, who still hadn't caught on.

"Not really," said Hercules. He picked up the golden apples. "See you, Atlas!" And he and his party started off toward Mycenae.

"Hey, wait!" called Atlas. "Come back! Come back! Awww, man!"

I felt sort of bad, tricking Atlas like that. But Hercules couldn't have stood that weight for very long. He would have collapsed, then the sky would have fallen, and what a mess that would have been.

"Coming with us to see the king, Hades?" asked Cee.

"No, I don't —" I stopped. "What's that funny smell?"

"Whoa!" said Hercules. He was staring at something on the south.

Orthus gave a deep, double growl.

I turned and saw what he saw. A dragon! It had many heads and many fang-filled mouths, all of which were open wide. It came slithering toward us.

"Uh-oh," said Cee. "Let's get out of here!"

But Hydra put out a hand to stop him. Then she waddled toward the dragon as fast as her little flipper feet could go. Orthus suddenly stopped growling. He bounded toward the dragon.

"Don't tell me," Cee said. "Another family reunion?"

Exactly. Ladon, the many-headed funky-smelling dragon, was Hydra and Orthus's brother. Once more, there was a festival of licking and hugging and tail wagging. Hydra signed to us that Ladon wished to go visit King Eurystheus with them. After Hercules gave the king the apples, Ladon planned on getting them back and taking them home to the garden of the Hesperides.

"Good luck, Hercules," I told him, giving him a godly slap on the back. "So, just one labor to go."

"Aren't you coming, Uncle Hades?" he asked.

"No, no," I said. "I have to get home. I know you can handle whatever the last labor is. And if you run into any problems . . ."

Hydra held up the little phone.

You see how I kept my promise to Persephone? I went straight back home. That night, my first lieutenant, Hypnos, built us a great fire in the fireplace. For the next few weeks, we sat in easy chairs each evening after supper, talking and reading. Sometimes the Furies joined us before they went out avenging. And every night Cerbie lay by the fire, resting his heads on his paws, snoring softly. We were the picture of contentment.

Then one night there was a knock at the door. I heard Hypnos hurrying down the hallway to answer it. A moment later, he poked his head in through the door of the den.

"Visitors, Lord Hades," he said. Then in a whisper, he added, "Mortals."

"More suitors for you, P-phone?" I joked as I got up out of my chair. "Cerbie, you stay and guard Persephone, just in case." I wondered what I'd done to Hermes that he had started telling mortals how they could get into my kingdom via my cave shortcut. I made a mental note to talk to him as I headed for the door, and to my great surprise, there stood Hercules!

"Hey there, Uncle Hades," he said. "Cool palace."

Beside him stood Cee and the three monsters.

"Come in," I said wearily. "Say hello to Persephone." And I led the way back to the den.

Persephone, as always, was the perfect hostess. She'd already called down to the kitchen and asked the serving ghosts to send up some snacks. Mortal food for Hercules and Cee. Ambrosia-laced snacks for Hydra, Orthus, and Ladon. She served them each a little plate, and they were all charmed by her.

Of course when Cerbie saw three of his siblings come waddling, bounding, and slithering into the den, he leapt for joy. Once more, there was much licking, etc. Cerbie was so much smaller than his sister and brothers, I figured he'd been the runt of the litter. Still, Cerbie suited me fine. I wouldn't have traded him for any big ferocious dog, no matter how many heads it had. Echidna's offspring ran and jumped and frolicked about so much that at last I opened the back door and shooed them all outside where they could behave like, well, monsters.

"All right," I said to Hercules and Cee when things had calmed down. "Why are you here?"

"Labor XII," said Cee.

"Ah," I said. "You have to bring King Eury something from my kingdom?"

Hercules nodded.

"Gems from my caves?" I asked. "Silver from my mines? Gold? Name it. It's yours.

"You won't like it," said Cee.

"I'm not overly attached to my possessions," I said. "Whatever I have, you take it."

"It's Cerberus," said Hercules. "King Eury wants your dog."

CHAPTER XX
BIG DOG

"No," I said. "He can't have my dog."

"Come on, Uncle Hades," said Hercules.

"No," I said again. "No, no, no, no, NO!"

"It's my last labor," Hercules told me. "I've got to take Cerbie to Eury."

"Over my dead body," I told him. And when an immortal says that, it means "never."

These mortals! First one wanted my queen. Now one wanted my dog. What was next, my wrestling girdle from the first Olympic games?

I was about to say NO again when the monsters scampered back in.

Hydra began signing, with Cee interpreting. Finally, Cee turned to me. "Hydra says Theseus is sitting out on the back porch."

"Theseus?" Hercules jumped up. "Is . . . is he a ghost?"

"No," I said. Truthfully, I'd forgotten all about those two, sitting in the Chair of Forgetfulness. "You want to see him? Come on." I led the way around the palace to the porch.

"Theseus!" exclaimed Hercules.

Theseus looked up, puzzled. "Who are you?" he asked.

Hercules turned to me. "What's wrong with him?"

I explained about the Chair of Forgetfulness. And why I'd put these mortals there.

"You must let Theseus go!" Hercules said. "Do it for me, Uncle Hades. Please!"

"All right," I said. "You can take Theseus. But his pal stays here. And so does Cerbie."

Hercules held out his hand to Theseus. I gave my permission, and the chair released him.

Theseus took a long look at Hercules. "I know you from somewhere," he said.

Hercules clapped him on the back. Then he turned to me. "Come on, Uncle Hades," he said.

"I have to do Labor XII. Let me have Cerberus. I'll take good care of him."

"All right, all right," I said. "But I'm coming too. And no way is that wimpy king keeping my dog."

I had to break it to Persephone that I was taking one more little trip up to earth.

Then I called the dog. "Come on, Cerbie! Want to go for a ride?"

This time, when Hercules and all his hangers-on walked through the gates of Mycenae, the crowd cheered, whistled, and stomped to honor him. Everyone knew that this was Hercules's final labor, and they'd come to cheer their favorite hero. And what a strange procession the hero and his posse made: two muscle-bound heroes (for Theseus had come along as well), a lion, and four monsters. I was there, too, but helmeted.

Hercules stopped outside the palace. "Eury!" he called. "Come and see Cerberus, guard dog of the Underworld. Come out! For I have finished my labors!"

The slot opened. "Where's the dog?" said Eury from inside the pot. "I can't see him."

"Go on, Cerbie," I gave him an invisible nudge. "Show yourself to the king."

"Where is he?" Eury was saying. "If I can't see him, it doesn't count. You will have failed, Hercules. XI out of XII labors just doesn't cut it."

Cerberus tilted his heads, listening, as the king ranted on and on. He stepped up to the big bronze pot. And then, before my eyes, Cerberus started growing. He grew and grew until he was X times his normal size! And still he kept expanding, like a huge dog balloon. His little paws grew to the size of a bear's feet, with long, menacing claws. Spikes popped out along his spine and all down his tail: *Pop! Pop! Pop! Pop! Pop! Pop! Pop! Pop!* Cerbie's six eyes glowed like red-hot coals as he peered down into the great bronze pot. Then he let out a triple growl that rattled the pot like an earthquake.

At this point, I was pretty sure I didn't have to worry about Eury wanting to keep my dog.

"Stop! No! Down, dogs!" whimpered Eury,

who must have been looking up from inside the pot. "Hercules? Call them off!"

"Not my dog," said Hercules.

Cerberus still towered over the pot.

"Don't eat me!" cried Eury. "I'll give you my servants! You can eat them!"

Cerbie shoved the pot with his front legs. The pot crashed over onto its side. Then Cerbie butted it with all three heads. The pot started rolling. It rolled slowly at first, but as it started rolling down the hill, it picked up speed. It rolled faster and faster and faster. Inside, Eury was yelling and screaming. The pot acted as a huge bronze megaphone, and his voice echoed so loudly that everyone for miles around could hear him shrieking and whimpering as he rolled down the mountain. The crowd stood still and watched the pot grow smaller and smaller as it rolled. Finally, it rolled off a cliff and splashed into the ocean, where it was quickly carried out to sea. And that was the last anyone saw of King Eurystheus. Ever.

I was so intent on watching the pot, that I missed seeing Cerbie shrink back down to his normal guard-dog-of-the-Underworld size. But later, Cee told me he looked very much like a balloon with a leak.

Now the crowd began to cheer for Hercules. He'd worked hard for years, and he'd completed XII all-but-impossible labors. Okay, he'd had a little help. But still, he was a big hero, and this was his big moment. He strutted outside the palace, waving, flexing his muscles, and generally showing off for all the other mortals.

Suddenly a bright white light flashed in front of the palace, and there stood Hera.

My godly heart sank. Could she not give him a few minutes to enjoy himself before she inflicted her next torture?

"Hercules," said Hera.

Hercules had enough sense to bow down to her.

"You have done well," Hera went on. "And you have suffered enough."

What? Could I believe my ears? Had Hera really said that?

"Because you have done so well at your

labors, I, Hera, have convinced the other XI Power Olympians that you are worthy to become an immortal."

"Awesome!" said Hercules.

"You may live up on Mount Olympus," Hera went on.

"Whoa," said Hercules.

If Hera loaded on one more good thing, she'd use up his entire vocabulary.

"And," said Hera, "you may have the hand of my own daughter, Hebe, in marriage."

Ah, here it was. I'd been waiting to see what Hera was going to get out of this. She was goddess of marriage, and she had an unmarried daughter. It must have been getting embarrassing.

"Oh, great and awesome goddess," said Hercules, not really sure how he should address her. "I thank you for your great gifts and generous offers. But —"

But? Now I *really* couldn't believe my ears.

"But," Hercules continued, "I chose the hard path. I have not walked all the way down it yet. There are more monsters to be slain. More mortals who still need the help of a hero like me." He grinned.

I was ready for Hera to slap XII more labors on him. But again, she surprised me.

"The deal stands," Hera told him. "When you are ready, send me word, and I shall keep my promise."

A white light flashed again, and Hera was gone.

As soon as she vanished, the crowd turned to Hercules and went totally crazy. I never knew mortals could make so much noise. Hercules had said no to immortality. He was going to stay on earth to help the little people. There's no better definition of a hero than that.

Now I understood that Hercules didn't need help from his Uncle Hades anymore. He'd be just fine on his own. I reached over and tapped him on the shoulder.

"It's been fun, Hercules," I told him. "Keep in touch."

"No problem, Uncle Hades," Hercules said. "And thanks. Thanks for everything."

I was sort of glad he didn't really know what "everything" was.

"Bye, Cee. Bye, Hydra," I said. "So long, Orthus and Ladon. Come on, Cerbie. Let's go." My dog made the rounds, saying goodbye to his siblings and then ran to my side. I picked him up and — *ZIP!* — we landed beside my chariot.

"Home, Harley! Home, Davidson!" I called, and I steered my steeds toward the cave shortcut to the Underworld. I was going home. And the next time I saw a cute baby, I planned to run away from it as fast as I could.

EPILOGUE

Now you know the T.R.U.T.H. about Hercules. Looking out for him until he grew up was a full-time job, and all that astro-traveling really wore me out. Too bad there weren't frequent-flyer miles back then. I would have racked up millions.

I was late finishing my first draft of *Get to Work, Hercules!*, so I sent the manuscript right to my publisher.

The next week, I grabbed my copy of *The Big Fat Book of Greek Myths* and went out to the back porch to see if I could find a myth for my next book.

"Hello, Peirithous," I said to the unfortunate mortal still sitting in the Chair of Forgetfulness.

He nodded happily but blankly, having no clue who I was. Or who he was, for that matter.

I sat down on my throne and started reading. I was so into the myths that when a knock sounded, I jumped a mile.

I stared as my sister Hestia, goddess of the hearth, walked in. She tended the fire up on Mount Olympus XXIV/VII. What was she doing in the Underworld? And what was she doing holding a copy of my *Hercules* manuscript?

"Hestia!" I said. "This is a surprise."

"You're probably wondering why I have your story, Hades," she said as she approached me. "The truth is, being goddess of the hearth is very solitary. I want to get out more, meet some gods, demi-gods, whatever. You think I want to stay single forever? No! So I got a job, Hades. I'm your new editor."

"You've . . . read my book?" I asked.

Hestia nodded. "It is a great story, Hades. But there are so many typos and spelling mistakes. Whole sections are impossible to read."

"I had a tight deadline," I muttered. "I was counting on the copy editors to fix it all up."

"They fixed it, Hades," said Hestia. "But they weren't happy about it." She started to sit down in the chair.

"Not there!" I cried.

"What?" Hestia jumped away from the chair. "Oh!" she said, noticing Peirithous for the first time.

"That's Peirithous," I said. "He's the mortal who came down here to woo Queen Persephone."

Hestia's eyes lit up. "I remember him from the story," she said. "The copy editors had a terrible time with his name. So he's been sitting in the Chair of Forgetfulness all these years?"

"Centuries," I said.

"I guess it serves him right, trying to steal your wife and all," said Hestia, taking a seat across from him. "Tell me, Hades, did Cee and all those monsters stay with Hercules when he went off to do more heroic deeds?"

"Cee stuck with him like honey dripping from a beehive," I told her. "But Hercules led a pretty rugged life. In time, Hydra, Orthus, and Ladon moved back home."

"Back to the cave that Echidna fixed up so nicely?" said Hestia.

"Right," I said. "At first, Echidna wasn't all that thrilled to have them back. But they were her kids. What could she do?"

"Anything you can add to this story?" asked Hestia.

"Hercules helped mortals," I said. "And he even helped a Titan — Prometheus. Remember how he —"

"Gave the guys fire?" Hestia finished for me. "How could I forget? It was my fire he stole, Hades. I thought he liked me, but no. He was only after my fire."

"Well, he was punished for it," I told her. "Zeus had Force and Violence chain him to a rock in the Caucasus Mountains, and he sent an eagle to tear out his liver."

"That's disgusting!" Hestia cried. "I mean, I was mad at Prometheus for using me and all, but he didn't deserve *that*!"

"The good news is that Hercules found Prometheus, chained to that rock," I told her.

"When he heard what his own father had done, it made him so angry that he grabbed Prometheus's chains, pulled with all his might, and broke them. He set Prometheus free."

"Really?" said Hestia. "Do you happen to know if Prometheus is seeing anybody special these days, Hades?"

"I don't," I said. "Ask Po. He knows all about the social scene."

"Po! Right." Hestia made a note to herself. "One more question. Did Hera keep her promise and make Hercules an immortal?"

"She did," I said.

"You might want to add that to your book," said Hestia. "And — do you happen to know if *he* is seeing anyone?"

"Hera fixed it so that he married her daughter, Hebe," I said.

Hestia sighed. "All the good immortals are taken."

"For my next book," I said, changing the subject, "I'm thinking about telling the story of Atalanta. She was an amazing mortal athlete."

"Stories about athletes sell," said Hestia. "But I've never heard of her."

"Read this, for starters." I passed her *The Big Fat Book of Greek Myths*.

ATALANTA HAD NO WISH TO MARRY, BUT HER FATHER SAID SHE MUST. SHE COULD RUN LIKE THE WIND, SO SHE SAID SHE'D MARRY A MAN ONLY IF HE COULD OUTRUN HER. MANY MEN CAME TO RACE HER AND LOST. BUT WHEN MELANION RAN, HE THREW GOLDEN APPLES INTO ATALANTA'S PATH. SHE STOPPED TO PICK THEM UP, AND MELANION WON THE RACE. THE TWO MARRIED AND LIVED HAPPILY EVER AFTER.

"Atalanta ran after the golden apples?" said Hestia. "She sounds greedy."

"She wasn't," I said. "Atalanta only wanted those golden apples so she could help a sick friend."

"Hold it," said Hestia. "Was Atalanta a goody-goody? Books about goody-goodies always end up in the '99¢ Special' bins."

"No way," I said. "Atalanta was raised by a bear. She could growl and wrestle and hunt like a champ. The only gold she cared about was winning an Olympic gold medal. I'm thinking of calling my book *Go For the Gold, Atalanta!*"

"Nice." Hestia stood up. "I have to get back to the office, Hades. Some editors are going out to Sky Bar after work, and you never know who you might meet at that kind of a get-together."

She hurried to the door, turning back to say, "It's another tight deadline. Get to work, Hades."

And so I did.

KING HADES'S
QUICK-AND-EASY
GUIDE TO THE MYTHS

Let's face it, mortals. When you read the Greek myths, you sometimes run into long, unpronounceable names like *Eurytheus* and *Stymphalian* — names so complicated that just looking at them can give you a great big headache. Not only that, but sometimes you mortals call us by our Greek names and other times by our Roman names. It can get pretty confusing. But never fear! I'm here to set you straight with my quick-and-easy guide to who's who and what's what in the myths.

Alcmene (alc-ME-nay) — princess of Thebes; briefly married to Zeus; mother of Hercules.

Alpheus (AL-fee-us) — a river god.

ambrosia (am-BRO-zha) — food that we gods must eat to stay young and good-looking for eternity.

Amphitryon (am-FIH-tree-on) — married Alcmene and became stepfather to Hercules.

Arcadia (are-KAY-dee-uh) — a large region in Greece.

Artemis (AR-tuh-miss) — goddess of the chase, the hunt, and the moon; Apollo's twin sister. The Romans call her *Diana*.

Athena (uh-THEE-nuh) — goddess of wisdom, weaving, and war; wears a Gorgon mask on the breastplate of her armor. The Romans call her *Minerva*.

Athens (ATH-enz) — important city in ancient Greece, sacred to Athena.

Atlas (AT-liss) — the biggest of the giant Titans; known for holding the sky on his shoulders.

Centaur (SEN-tor) — one of the race of monsters having the head, arms, and torso of a man and the body and legs of a horse.

Cerberus (SIR-buh-rus) — my fine, III-headed pooch; guard dog of the Underworld; for Labor

XII, Hercules was to capture Cerberus and bring him up from the Underworld.

Ceryneian Hind (sir-EE-nee-an HINDE) — the doe with golden antlers and hooves of brass that Hercules was to capture for Labor III; otherwise known as Precious.

Charon (CARE-un) — river-taxi driver; ferries the living and the dead across the River Styx.

Cretan Bull (KREE-tin) — a bull Hercules had to capture for Labor VII.

Delphi (DELL-fie) — an oracle in Greece on the southern slope of Mount Parnassus where a sibyl is said to predict the future.

Demeter (duh-MEE-ter) — my sister; goddess of agriculture and total gardening nut. The Romans call her *Ceres*.

Eurymanthian Boar (your-ee-MAN-the-an) — the wild boar that Hercules was to slay for Labor IV.

Eurystheus (your-ISS-thee-us) — king of Mycenae; conniving with Hera, he gave Hercules the XII Labors to perform.

Furies (FYOOR-eez) — three winged immortals with red eyes and serpents for hair who pursue and punish wrongdoers.

Geryon (GAIR-yon) — self-proclaimed Strongest Man in the World, Geryon had two legs, one set of hips, three torsos, six arms, and three heads; Hercules was to fetch his herd of red cattle to complete Labor X.

Hades (HEY-deez) — Ruler of the Underworld, Lord of the Dead, King Hades, that's me. I'm also god of wealth, owner of all the gold, silver, and precious jewels in the earth. The Romans call me *Pluto*.

Helios (HEE-lee-ohss) — sun god; drives the chariot of the sun from east to west across the sky each day; son of Hyperion.

Hera (HERE-uh) — my sister; Queen of the Olympians; goddess of marriage; the Romans call her *Juno*. I call her "The Boss."

Hercules (HER-kew-leez) — Roman name of the son of Zeus and Alcmene; a major, muscle-bound hero; won immortality by performing XII labors concocted by Hera; his name means "Glory of Hera." The Greeks call him *Heracles*.

Hermes (HER-meez) — messenger of the gods; also god of business executives, inventors, and thieves; escorts dead mortals down to the Underworld. The Romans call him *Mercury*.

Hesperides (hess-PAIR-uh-deez) — the daughters of the Titan Atlas; they tend a garden on the slope of Mount Atlas where a tree belonging to Hera that bears golden apples grows; for Labor XI, Hercules was to fetch these golden apples.

Hippolyta (hip-AW-lit-uh) — Queen of the Amazons; Hercules was to get her golden girdle, a gift from Ares, to complete Labor IX.

Hydra (HI-dra) — nine-headed monster; daughter of Typhon and Echidna. Hercules was to slay her as Labor II.

Hypnos (HIP-nos) — god of sleep; brother of Thanatos (the god of death); son of Nyx, or night; my first lieutenant in the Underworld.

immortal (i-MOR-tuhl) — a being, such as a god or possibly a monster, who will never die, like me.

Ladon (LAY-don) — a monstrous dragon: guard of Hera's apple tree in the garden of the Hesperides; offspring of Echidna and Typhon.

Linus (LIE-nus) — one of Hercules's teachers.

Lion of Cithaeron (SITH-air-on) — lion reputed to ravage cattle herds that Hercules supposedly offed. We know better. Also known as Cee.

Mares of Diomedes (MAIRZ OV die-o-MEE-deez) — horses fed on human flesh and made monstrous by King Diomedes; for Labor VIII, Hercules was to capture them.

mortal (MOR-tuhl) — a being who one day must die. I hate to be the one to break this to you, but *you* are a mortal.

Mount Olympus (oh-LIM-pess) — the highest mountain in Greece; home to all the major gods, except for my brother Po and me.

nectar (NECK-ter) — what we gods like to drink; has properties that invigorate us and make us look good and feel godly.

Nemean Lion (neh-MEE-an) — an enormous lion whose pelt could not be pierced by any weapon of iron, bronze, or stone. Hercules was to kill it as Labor I.

oracle (OR-uh-kull) — a sacred place where a seer or sibyl is said to foretell the future; the sibyl and her prophecy are also called oracles.

Orthus (OR-thus) — II-headed dog belonging to Geryon; monstrous offspring of Typhon and Echidna.

Peirithous (peh-RITH-oh-us) — a mortal who went to the Underworld to woo Queen Persephone; ended up sitting in the Chair of Forgetfulness.

Peneius (peh-NAY-us) — a river god.

Persephone (per-SEF-uh-knee) — goddess of spring and my Queen of the Underworld. The Romans call her *Proserpina*.

Polyhymnia (poh-lee-HIM-nee-uh) — muse of music.

Poseidon (po-SIGH-den) — my bro Po; god of the seas, rivers, lakes, and earthquakes; one of the XII Power Olympians; actual father of Theseus by his short-term wife, Aethra; the Romans call him *Neptune*.

Roman numerals (ROH-muhn NOO-mur-uhlz) — what the ancients used instead of counting on their fingers.

I	1	XI	11	XXX	30
II	2	XII	12	XL	40
III	3	XIII	13	L	50
IV	4	XIV	14	LX	60
V	5	XV	15	LXX	70
VI	6	XVI	16	LXXX	80
VII	7	XVII	17	XC	90
VIII	8	XVIII	18	C	100
IX	9	XIX	19	D	500
X	10	XX	20	M	1000

sibyl (SIB-ul) — a mortal woman said to be able to foretell the future; a prophetess.

Stables of Augeias (aw-GUY-us) —
unbelievably flithy stables that Hercules
had to muck out to complete Labor V.

Stymphalian birds (stim-FAIL-ee-un) —
huge iron-clawed, iron-beaked, iron-winged,
stinky birds that Hercules had to get rid of for
Labor VI.

Thebes (THEEBZ) — city in ancient Greece,
northwest of Athens.

Theseus (THEE-see-us) — a great hero of
ancient Athens who is known for never
taking the easy way out and, mistakenly,
for slaying the Minotaur; accompanied his
friend Pirithous to the Underworld; sat in
the Chair of Forgetfulness until rescued by
Hercules.

Titan (TIGHT-un) — any of the twelve giant
children of Gaia and Uranus.

Underworld (UHN-dur-wurld) — my very
own kingdom, where the ghosts of dead
mortals come to spend eternity.

Zeus (ZOOSE) — rhymes with *goose*, which pretty much says it all; my little brother, a major myth-o-maniac and a cheater, who managed to set himself up as Ruler of the Universe. The Romans call him *Jupiter*.

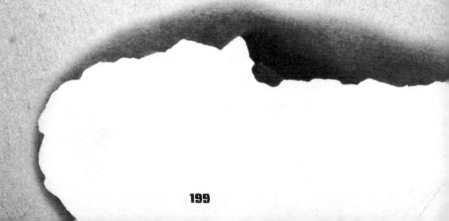

THE BIG FAT BOOK
OF GREEK MYTHS

Hercules was the greatest of all the heroes in Greek mythology. He was the strongest man on earth and considered himself equal to the gods.

Hercules was born the mortal son of Zeus, king of the gods, and Alcmene, a mortal woman. Unfortunately, Zeus's queen, Hera, was jealous of Hercules. When he was still a baby, she sent two serpents into his crib to kill him. But like Zeus, Hercules had the courage of a lion and the strength of a bull. He was found with a strangled snake in each hand, laughing happily.

Even though Hercules grew up, Hera continued to hold a grudge against him, and she drove him crazy. In a fit of insanity, Hercules tragically killed his wife and children. As punishment for the terrible crime, Hercules was assigned XII labors. He was sentenced to perform these labors for his cousin, King Eurystheus.

The XII Labors of Hercules were:

1. *Slay the Nemean Lion*

2. *Slay the nine-headed Lernaean Hydra*

3. *Capture the Golden Hind of Artemis*

4. *Capture the Erymanthian Boar*

5. *Clean the Augean stables in a single day*

6. *Slay the Stymphalian Birds*

7. *Capture the Cretan Bull*

8. *Steal the Mares of Diomedes*

9. *Obtain the girdle of Hippolyta, Queen of the Amazons*

10. *Obtain the cattle of the monster Geryon*

11. *Steal the apples of the Hesperides*

12. *Capture and bring back Cerberus*

Each labor would have been impossible for a normal mortal. It took Hercules XII years, but he completed all XII labors. Hercules was the greatest hero Greece has ever known. When he died, he became the only hero to join the gods on Mount Olypmus as an immortal.

KATE McMULLAN is the author of the chapter book series Dragon Slayers' Academy, as well as easy readers featuring Fluffy, the Classroom Guinea Pig. She and her illustrator husband, Jim McMullan, have created several award-winning picture books, including *I STINK!*, *I'M DIRTY!*, and *I'M BIG!* Her latest work is *SCHOOL! Adventures at Harvey N. Trouble Elementary* in collaboration with the famed *New Yorker* cartoonist George Booth. Kate and Jim live in Sag Harbor, NY, with two bulldogs and a mews named George.

GLOSSARY

chariot (CHAIR-ee-uht) — a small vehicle pulled by a horse, used in ancient times for battle or races

dreary (DRIHR-ee) — dull and miserable

gnarled (NAR-uhld) — twisted and lumpy with age

horde (HORD) — a large, noisy, moving crowd of people or animals

majestic (muh-JESS-tik) — having great power and beauty

pennant (PEN-uhnt) — a long, triangular flag, often with the name of a school or team on it

proclamation (prok-luh-MAY-shuhn) — a public and official announcement

scheme (SKEEM) — a plot or plan for doing something

suspicious (suh-SPISH-uhss) — thinking that something is wrong or bad, but having little or no proof to back up your feelings

suitor (SOO-tur) — a man who courts a woman

DISCUSS!

I. Talk about the XII Labors of Hercules. Which labor do you think was the easiest? Which was the hardest? Explain your answers.

II. Hercules is one of ancient Greece's most famous heroes. Talk about some other ancient heroes you've heard of.

III. Hercules had a lot of help on his adventures. Which sidekick do you think was the most helpful? Discuss your reasons.

WRITE!

I. Hercules's friends help him with the XII Labors Hera assigned him. Write about a time one of your friends helped you with an adventure of some kind.

II. Hera disliked Hercules from the beginning, just because he was Zeus's son. Write about a time someone treated you unfairly.

III. If you were in charge of Hercules's labors, what would you have made him do? Write your own list of XII Labors.

MYTH·O·MANIA

HAVE A HOT TIME, HADES!

Kate McMullan

I

PHONE HOME, PERSEPHONE!

Kate McMullan

II

STOP THAT BULL, THESEUS!

Kate McMullan

V

KEEP A LID ON IT, PANDORA!

Kate McMullan

VI

READ THE WHOLE SERIES AND LEARN THE **REAL** STORIES!

III

IV

VII

VIII

THE FUN DOESN'T STOP HERE!

DISCOVER MORE:

Videos & Contests!
Games & Puzzles!
Heroes & Villains!
Authors & Illustrators!

@ www.CAPSTONEKIDS.com

Find cool websites and more books
like this one at WWW.FACTHOUND.COM.
Just type in Book I.D. 9781434231963
and you're ready to go!